D1565407

Lucretia Mott

Lucretia Mott

By Dorothy Sterling

THE FEMINIST PRESS AT THE CITY UNIVERSITY OF NEW YORK
NEW YORK

Published by The Feminist Press at The City University of New York
City College, Wingate Hall, Convent Avenue at 138th Street, New York, NY 10031
www.feministpress.org

First paperback edition, 1999

First published in 1964 by Doubleday & Company, Inc., Garden City, New York.

Library of Congress Cataloging-in-Publication Data

Sterling, Dorothy, 1913–
    [Lucretia Mott, gentle warrior]
    Lucretia Mott / by Dorothy Sterling
        p.   cm.
    Originally published: Lucretia Mott, gentle warrior. Garden City, N.Y. : Doubleday,
1964.
    Includes bibliographical references.
    Summary: Biography of the nineteenth-century New England woman who was the
Quaker daughter of a Nantucket sea captain and who fought for the abolition of slav-
ery and for women's rights.
    ISBN 1-55861-217-3 (alk. paper)
    1. Mott, Lucretia, 1793–1880—Juvenile literature. 2. Women abolitionists—United
States—Biography—Juvenile literature. 3. Abolitionists—United States—Biography—
Juvenile literature. 4. Feminists—United States—Biography—Juvenile literature. 5.
Quakers—United States—Biography—Juvenile literature. [1. Mott, Lucretia, 1793–1880.
2. Abolitionists. 3. Feminists. 4. Quakers. 5. Women—Biography.] I. Title.
E449.M93S8 1999
305.42'092—dc21
[B]   98-52881
                                                                                    CIP
                                                                                     AC

Publication of this book was made possible, in part, by a grant from the Ford
Foundation. The Feminist Press gratefully acknowledges the Ford Foundation for its
support. The Feminist Press is also grateful to Joanne Markell and Genevieve Vaughan
for their generosity in supporting this publication.

Printed on acid-free paper by Transcontinental Printing
Printed in Canada

05 04 03 02 01 00 99   5 4 3 2 1

They are slaves who dare not be
In the right with two or three.

JAMES RUSSELL LOWELL

Contents

Lucretia Mott

COFFIN-MOTT FAMILY TREE

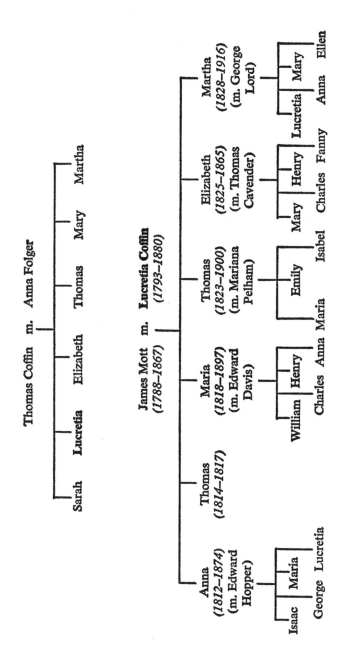

1. The Beginning

My ancestors were fine, long men,
Their hands were like square sails,
They ran the lengths of longitudes,
Harpooning spouting whales.
ROBERT P. TRISTRAM COFFIN

The weather vane on the roof top came about smartly in the January wind. All along the street, shutters banged and panes of glass rattled in their leaded frames. Thomas Coffin paced the room restlessly. After stirring up the fire and smiling absently at little Sarah, he wandered over to the window again.

Now that the wind was blowing away the fog, he could see the outlines of ships bobbing at anchor in the bay. From Straight Wharf a longboat laden with stores was putting out for the *Hepzibah*. She would be ready to sail tomorrow if the wind held. If the wind held and Anna was all right.

Abruptly he walked from the window to the foot of the stairs. Dropping her rag doll, Sarah trotted after him. Together they listened to the *tap tap* of footsteps overhead. Then they heard it again—the high-pitched wail of a baby.

Thomas took the steps two at a time. In the big front bedroom old Rachael Bunker was wrapping a tiny form in layer after layer of muslin and soft quilting.

"A girl," she grunted. "Mighty skinny. I hope thou'll be able to raise her."

"Anna?" Thomas tiptoed toward the bed where his wife was dozing. She had a tired smile on her face.

"Well enough." Rachael had few words to waste. "If thou will hold the baby, I'll go down to make some tea."

Thomas seated himself awkwardly on the cane-bottomed chair by the fire with the bundled-up baby on his lap. This new daughter of his certainly didn't look like much. A tuft of dark hair, a wrinkled red face, a balled-up fist waving aimlessly.

"Father—" Sarah tugged at his breeches.

"See the baby. Look at thy new sister."

Sarah poked a curious forefinger at the wriggling bundle and was rewarded with a cry. At just that moment, Rachael returned with a steaming kettle in her hand.

"Mullein tea. Best thing for them both. Give her here now."

With a relieved nod, Thomas handed the baby to Rachael and walked to the window. The harbor was buzzing with activity.

Anna stirred, murmuring as if she were talking in her sleep. Thomas knelt beside the bed so that he could hear her.

"The wind," she whispered. "With this wind, the *Hepzibah* will be able to go out on the tide tomorrow."

"I can't leave thee alone." Thomas shook his head. "Hast thou forgotten? Rachael has to go on Fourth day."

"Thou must leave." Anna's eyes flew open and she struggled to sit up. "What would Nantucket say for a husband not to sail when his ship was ready? Now that the fog is lifting, thou can fetch Mother. We'll manage."

She would manage, of course. Nantucket women were used to managing when their husbands were at sea. When wind and tide were right, not even a new baby could delay a ship's sailing.

The Coffins named their second daughter Lucretia. When she was born, on January 3, 1793, George Washington was President and there were fifteen stars in the flag that floated above Congress Hall in Philadelphia. In that same cold month, General Anthony Wayne led bluecoated troops against the Indians in the Northwest Territory. Eli Whitney, on a fateful visit to Georgia, was tinkering with his first cotton gin. Across the ocean, King Louis XVI of France listened to his subjects' cries of *"Liberty, Equality, Fraternity!"* as a cart carried him to the guillotine.

It was a time of change. The new Union of States was growing. The Old World was making itself over. It was a good time to be born and Nantucket was a good place.

More than a hundred years earlier, twenty Englishmen, headed by Tristram Coffin, had bought the island from the Indians for thirty pounds sterling and two beaver hats. The Indians called it "The Faraway Island" because it was thirty watery miles from the Massachusetts mainland. It's hard to guess what Coffin and his fellows were looking for when they left a fruitful continent for this windswept, fogbound sandbank. Perhaps it was those thirty miles that attracted them—a chance to live far from the autocratic rulers of the Massachusetts Bay Colony.

Nantucket was covered with scrub oak and poverty grass and cranberry vine. Not much could be raised there except sheep—and people. But there were fruits in the waters around, clam and cod and herring, and that giant of the sea, the sperm whale.

After the Indians had taken the white men whaling in their bark canoes, there was no holding Nantucket. Its settlers plowed the sea instead of the land. In ships hardly bigger than their prey, they sailed north to the Arctic Circle and east to the Guinea Coast and beyond. Before long, their sperm candles and whale oil lamps were bringing light to the homes of Europe and America.

Sheep and whales—and people. It wasn't a bad crop for a fogbound crook of land only fifteen miles long. Nor were the people the least part of the crop. The first settlers reaped a harvest of sturdy men, captains and pilots, coopers and ropemakers, blacksmiths, merchants, teachers. And Nantucket women were as able as their mates. With their husbands at sea for two years at a time, wives learned to keep accounts and transact business as well as take charge of their families.

Folks said that Nantucket whalemen set sail with a harpoon in one hand and a Bible in the other. Yet even in religion they were independent of the mainland. The first settlers on Nantucket had no church. After fifty years on the island, they built a Friends Meeting House.

Of all the groups seeking to reform the Church of England, the Society of Friends was the most radical. Rejecting the ceremonies of the established church, Friends sought to live the simple lives of early Christians. The depth of their religious feeling, which caused them to tremble as they preached, won for them the derisive name of "Quaker."

Puritan New England reacted violently to the Friends' preaching. In the year that Nantucket was settled, two Friends were hanged on Boston Common. Two more, one of them a woman, were executed in following years. But this persecution gradually came to an end. After Pennsylvania was founded by William Penn as a Quaker colony, Friends traveled up the Atlantic coast holding meetings wherever a door was opened to them.

There were several such doors on Nantucket. The simple, direct faith of the Quakers appealed to the hard-working island community. By the time of the American Revolution, there were two Quaker meetings on the island and more than half of the inhabitants were Friends.

During the fight for independence, the men and women of Nantucket saw hard times. Their ships were captured and their stores of oil and flour confiscated by British and Americans alike. In the darkest days of the war, the hungry islanders talked seriously of setting up a republic of their own.

By 1793, these days seemed far behind. Now the countries of Europe were at war and American ships were free to sail the seven seas. For the first time, a Nantucket square-rigger had rounded Cape Horn and sailors from the little island were hunting whales in the uncharted waters of the Pacific and beginning to talk of the China trade.

2. The House on Fair Street

At home the tender minds of the children must be early struck with the gravity, the serious, though cheerful deportment of their parents. They are corrected with tenderness, nursed with most affectionate care, clad with that decent plainness from which they observe their parents never to depart.
HECTOR ST. JOHN DE CRÈVECŒUR 1782

By the time the *Hepzibah* returned from the Brazil Banks loaded to the scuppers with sperm oil, Lucretia had graduated from cradle to trundle bed. Her first memories were of her parents' gray-shingled house on Fair Street. It was the kind of house a ship's carpenter would build—strong and square, with an oak frame and pine floors and paneling.

Although there were wooden shutters at the windows instead of curtains and the walls were bare of pictures, the high-ceilinged rooms were big and cheerful. In most New England homes of that time, parlor floors were spread with layers of sand. In the Coffins' house on sandy Nantucket, the wide floor boards were covered with bright rag carpeting which was taken up in summer and laid down again in the fall.

Lucretia and Sarah shared the back bedroom on the second floor. In winter they were up before the sun, washing in a bowl of icy water and dressing by candlelight. Breakfast was cooked over the open fireplace in the cellar while bread baked in the brick Dutch oven that was built into the fireplace wall.

Lucretia had taken her first baby steps in the cellar, pulling herself up on shelves crowded with preserves and balancing on the flour barrel or the sack of potatoes in the corner. She was small for her age, in spite of frequent doses of mullein tea, but she was a bundle of energy ceaselessly exploring her world.

She scalded her hands on the black iron pot while her mother was making soap. She splashed her dress at the pump in the yard and skinned her knuckles on the wire-covered paddle that was used for carding wool. She raised an egg-sized bump on her head when she tumbled down the attic stairs.

Once she walked all the way to Pleasant Street before anyone realized that she was missing. When her worried mother punished her by sending her to her room, Lucretia's gray eyes grew black with anger and she stamped her tiny feet.

"She's a spirited one," Grandmother Folger said.

"Stubborn," Anna corrected her.

Spirited and stubborn, Lucretia grew up quickly. She had little choice. Before her second birthday a new sister, Elizabeth, slept in the cradle in the front bedroom and Sarah teased, "Thou art not the baby any more." Three years later when brother Thomas was born her mother was glad to make use of Lucretia's eager fingers and wiry legs.

She learned to dust and to sweep and to dip water from the bucket without spilling it. She brought in logs and carried out slops and rocked the cradle if Thomas cried. She could tend the corn bread as it sputtered on the hearth and stir the chowder to keep it from burning. If Mother would only let her, she was sure that she could make blackberry pudding.

In the late afternoon when housework was done and visitors knocked at the door, Lucretia and Sarah raced each other for the privilege of letting them in. Long before she could see over the tops of the ladder-backed chairs, Lucretia liked to push them toward the parlor fire and urge the company to sit down. The chairs had to be arranged just right, in a sociable half-circle around the hearth. Then she would squeeze alongside Sarah on the settle and listen to the grownups' chatter.

Most of the Coffins' visitors were relatives. In fact, it was hard *not* to be related to the Coffins, if you lived on Nantucket, for the first Tristram had had seven children and sixty grandchildren. And Coffins had married Macys and Macys had married Starbucks and Starbucks had married Husseys and Husseys had married Gardiners and Gardiners had married Folgers and all of them had had such big families that Lucretia was out of breath long before she finished counting up her uncles and her cousins and her aunts.

She never knew Grandfather Coffin. He had been a school teacher who taught himself Latin and then painstakingly passed his knowledge along to a generation of island boys and girls. But her mother's parents, William and Ruth Folger, were very much alive. A descendant of Peter Folger, another of the island's first settlers, Grandfather Folger had been a prosperous shipowner until his vessels were seized during the Revolution. A stanch supporter of the British, he was still known as "Tory Bill." His neighbors laughed because Tory Bill wasn't above letting people know that Benjamin Franklin, the patriot leader, was his cousin, thrice removed. Declaration of Independence notwithstanding, Franklin's mother was a Folger, born right on Nantucket.

Grandfather Folger lived on a farm near Siasconset, a fishing village on the eastern shore of the island, but Mother's four brothers and five sisters were all close by.

When their husbands were at sea there was seldom a day that Aunt Phoebe or Aunt Elizabeth or Aunt Barker failed to drop in. Armed with gingham bags stuffed with yarn, or scraps of cloth for quilts and carpeting, the aunts' busy fingers kept pace with their wagging tongues.

Lucretia sat alongside them, her short legs hooked around the rungs of her chair as she struggled over the hem of a sampler or tried to knit a stocking with her mother's speed and skill. As the room grew dark, she hurried to light the candles with a glowing splinter of wood from the fire. If the aunts were staying for supper, Anna sometimes allowed her to light the little pewter lamp shaped like Aladdin's that had a place of honor on the mantelpiece. But even on Nantucket, whale oil was a precious commodity. More often than not, the women ate and talked by the soft glow of candle and firelight.

The calm of Lucretia's petticoat world was shattered once or twice a year by the clang of the town crier's bell. From the moment that he appeared on the street swinging his bell and chanting "Ship's at the bar!" all housework stopped. Bumping into each other in their excitement, Lucretia and Sarah ran to the hall cupboard for the spyglass and then headed up the stairs. With Thomas in her arms and Elizabeth at her heels, Anna dashed after them. On the narrow steps which led from the attic to the roof, she reached over the girls' heads to push open the scuttle. Then everyone scrambled out onto the walk, the railed-in platform on the roof from which they could see the blue waters of Nantucket Sound.

A schooner was rounding Brant Point. Was it Father's?

While the breathless girls jumped up and down, Anna pointed the spyglass at the incoming ship. Sails, rigging, the triangular captain's flag flying from the foremast—did they look familiar?

"It's thy father's." With a broad smile, she handed the glass to each child in turn.

It took two hands to hold the long spyglass. Lucretia pressed it tightly against her eye and tried to decide which of the tiny figures on the deck of the ship was Father. Before she could make up her mind, Anna was shooing them down the stairs. Bustling from room to room, she barked nervous orders as if she too were a ship's captain.

"Thou, Sarah, light the Dutch oven. Thy father will have had his fill of sea biscuit . . . Thou, Lucretia, polish the candlesticks . . . Thou, Elizabeth, fetch the kindling . . ."

Floors that had been swept that morning were swept again. Mantelpieces were dusted, lamps and wood bins filled. Sewing was put away in the small front parlor and a fresh fire laid in the big one.

At last they were ready. With bonnets neatly tied and shawls around their shoulders, Lucretia and her sisters ran on ahead. Straight Wharf was crowded but someone lifted Lucretia to the top of an oil cask so that she would have a better view of the harbor.

A fishing boat rowed out to meet the incoming ship. "What luck?" an oarsman called.

"Chock full!" a sailor shouted through a speaking trumpet. "All alive and well."

All well! Lucretia could hear the relieved sighs of the waiting women.

Soon Father, sunburned and smiling, strode down the gangplank. At first he looked different, somehow, than Lucretia remembered him, but by the time they reached home, the strangeness was gone. While she pushed his chair close to the fire, Sarah teased him to open his sea chest.

There were presents for everyone in the leatherbound chest—bright oranges and hairy coconuts and a curving pink and white conch shell. When Lucretia held the shell to her ear, she could hear the sea and the roar of wind.

"The Caribbean Sea. The trade winds," Father said.

She would have liked to ask him what he meant but her mother was calling from the kitchen. Ordinarily, Anna's cooking was like her house. She served solid, no-nonsense fare—hominy soup for breakfast, corn pudding for lunch, fish chowder or corned beef for supper. "Nantucket wives contrive to get along on what they have," she often said. But this was no ordinary day. Tonight she was making Indian dumplings and quahog pie to go with the chowder that was simmering over the fire. And tomorrow—tomorrow they would have a veal feast!

"And if thou art a good helpful girl," she promised Lucretia in her matter-of-fact way, "thou shall see them kill the calf."

Lucretia could scarcely sleep that night. Early in the morning she and Sarah left the house with Father. After trudging along the sandy trail to Grandfather's farm, they returned home in triumph in the Folgers' calash, a two-wheeled cart. The butchered calf was at their feet. For the rest of the day, they watched and helped and begged for tastes as Mother transformed the meat into cutlets and roasts and golden-brown pies.

A veal feast meant more than just good things to eat. With fresh meat scarce on the island, the killing of a calf was always followed by a two-day family reunion. The first evening the Coffin relatives came to dinner. The next it was the Folgers' turn—with a sprinkling of Macys, Starbucks, and Husseys crowding into the house as well. Lucretia hopped up and down, her eyes bright and her face flushed, as the circle of chairs in front of the hearth—her circle—grew and grew.

The women knitted. The men whittled. And Father told them about his voyage and listened to their news from the mainland and home. As the talk ranged from President John Adams and the Federalists to the danger of war with France, Lucretia's eyes closed and her head slowly tipped forward. Then Father called a halt to the conversation while he carried her up the stairs to bed.

3. First Lessons

I always loved the good, in childhood desired to do the right and prayed for strength to overcome a naturally quick temper.

LUCRETIA MOTT

At the Dame's school up the lane, Lucretia swayed from side to side chanting with her classmates, "One and one are two. Two and two are four. Three and three are six." She learned her letters from *The New England Primer,* starting with

> In Adam's fall
> We sinned all

and working down to

> Zaccheus he
> Did climb a tree
> His Lord to see.

After the primer had been mastered, she moved on to a Cent School where lessons were paid for at the rate of a penny a day. Arithmetic consisted of "sums" and reading and writing were taught by the copybook method. With homemade ink and a quill pen that her teacher showed her how to sharpen she copied again and again:

> *Avoid idleness*
> *Acquire virtuous habits*
> *Associate with the wise*

and

> Blame no one unheard
> Be deaf to distraction
> Bad company ruins many

She was never given pictures to color or stories to read or arithmetic problems to solve. School meant endless drill and endless memorizing. When she was seventy-five she could still write out in a neat hand an alphabetical acrostic she had learned on Nantucket:

> All mortal men that live must surely die
> But how, or when, is hid from human eye.
> Consider then, thy few uncertain days
> Delay no longer to amend thy ways.
> Engage thy heart to serve the Lord in love,
> For all his ways do ways of comfort prove
> Grant to thyself no time for vain delight
> Hate all that's wrong, and try to do the right . . .

She was a quick worker and after she had completed her task she was obliged to sit with folded hands while her slower classmates struggled with theirs. Although she tried to do the right, boredom often put an end to her good resolutions.

When Cousin Mary stumbled over the same word for the tenth time, Lucretia couldn't keep quiet any longer. She groaned out loud or imitated Mary under her breath until the girls sitting nearby were convulsed with giggles.

Then the teacher would pounce on her. "Lucretia, I'll have no more of thy teasing . . . Lucretia, thou must sit on the repentance stool until thou learns to behave." In her first years at school she spent more time on the high repentance stool than she cared to tell her mother about.

School was not the only place where Lucretia had trouble sitting still. The Friends' meeting house on Main Street was

a bare, undecorated room, cold in winter, hot and airless
in the summertime. Its whitewashed benches were hard.
Their straight backs and unpadded seats offered little comfort to Lucretia's short, thin body.

Invariably, she squirmed around. By leaning forward
she could look through a forest of gray bonnets to the
raised facing bench up front where the elders sat. If she
tilted her head she could see the men across the aisle, stiff
and serious in their homespun suits and tall beaver hats. But
soon her mother's warning hand would close over hers and
she would slump back. Swinging her legs she waited im-
patiently for someone to break the silence.

In the back of the room a man stood up, hat in hand.
He "felt a concern to speak," he said. Hesitantly, he recited a verse from the Bible. After that there was silence
again. Then came a woman with "a conviction to utter a
word." "Are Friends careful to live within the bounds of
their circumstances?" she asked. "Are there not some among
us who are wasting their pennies on frumpery?"

More silence. Lucretia wriggled and Anna frowned. At
last an elder rose from the facing bench and shook hands
with the women in front of him. "How art thou?" "How
dost thou do?" he asked. It was the signal for the end of the
meeting. The once-quiet room buzzed with noise as Friends
stretched their legs and greeted their neighbors.

In other New England churches of the day, boys and
girls sat on equally hard benches in almost as bare rooms,
listening to warnings of hell fire and damnation. "Man is
born wicked," their ministers thundered. "He lives a wicked
life. He will die without grace and suffer torment in Hell."

Friends' services were different. Because they believed
that every man had an "inner light" which could lead him
to God, they had no paid ministers. Their meetings were

silent until a member felt moved to speak. Sometimes a Friend who spoke unusually well became a preacher and sat on the elders bench. But even these preachers talked only when prompted by an "inner voice" and never received pay for their work.

Puritan youngsters left church on Sundays with bowed heads and a belief in their own unworthiness. They went home to dream of red-suited devils with pitchforks and scorching brimstone fires. The Quaker children were introduced to a God of love and hope rather than a God of wrath. The "inner voices" spoke of the here-and-now rather than the hereafter. As Lucretia began to listen on First days, the speakers often seemed to be directing questions at her.

"Dost thou control thy temper?" "Art thou patient?" "Dost thou practice plainness of speech and apparel?"

Once a visiting Friend, a woman preacher, told the story of Joseph whose brothers had sold him into slavery in Egypt. Lucretia was thoughtful as she walked down Fair Street after the meeting. She wanted to be as strong and brave as Joseph had been. She wanted to find a way to show her newfound strength.

Upstairs in her room she took stock of herself. What could she do to show that she was living by Quaker principles? Her simple dress and white kerchief and cap could scarcely be improved on. When her eyes traveled to her feet, she knew the answer.

She had bows on her shoes, bright blue bows that Uncle Mayhew had brought her from the mainland. Quickly, without giving herself a chance to change her mind, she found a pair of scissors and snipped off the bows. Then, because she was bossy as well as brave, she set about convincing her sisters that they must do likewise.

The Quakers lived in a world of their own, set apart by clothes and speech from "the world's people." They tried to make "Friend" mean a community of friends, with each taking an interest in his neighbor's welfare. On Nantucket the Friends organized schools for their children, took care of their sick and gave freely to the needy. They held monthly business meetings at which they recorded births, approved marriages, and appointed elders and preachers. Even arguments between Friends were settled at these meetings "in a brotherly and loving manner."

In addition to monthly and quarterly business meetings, they met once each year with Friends from other communities to discuss broader issues that were of interest to them all. Women as well as men took part in these discussions, which ranged from the need for "wakeful attendance" on First days and the dangers of novel-reading, to a concern for the condition of Indians and black slaves.

When meetings were held on Nantucket, the Coffins' house was filled to overflowing with off-islanders. At bedtime, the children were sent up to the attic to sleep. In the high-raftered attic, Lucretia liked to entertain an audience of sisters, brother, and cousins with imitations of the grownups' speeches. One evening Anna overheard one of her orations as she came up the stairs to say good night. Hiding a smile, she patted her daughter's shoulder.

"Thou speaks well, long tongue," she said. "Maybe thou will be a preacher some day."

4. Wider Worlds

*I can remember how our mothers were employed
while our fathers were at sea. At that time it required some money and some courage to get to Boston. They were obliged to go to that city, make their
trades, exchange their oils and candles for dry
goods, set their own price, keep their own accounts.*
LUCRETIA MOTT

Lucretia was seven, with a new baby sister named Mary,
when her father came home with big news. He had bought
a ship. Until then he had captained vessels belonging to his
older brothers. Now he was owner and commander of the
Tryal. On his first voyage under his own ensign, Captain
Coffin planned to sail along the southernmost shores of South
America hunting for seals. From there he would cross the
Pacific to barter sealskins for the silks and teas of China.

"China!" Aunt Barker said.

"Thou will be gone three years," Aunt Phoebe added.

"That is, if—" Aunt Mary left her sentence hanging in
midair.

Lucretia stole a glance at her mother. Three years was
more than twice as long as Father's other voyages—and
what did Aunt Mary mean by "if"? But the calm expression
on Anna's face never changed.

"The *Oneida,* out of New York, made the China trip in
seventeen months," Father told the aunts. "Would thou like
a China tea set, Anna?"

The *Tryal* was the first Nantucket ship to sail to China.

Thomas Coffin spent busy months outfitting her. She was anchored at Woods Hole on Cape Cod, because she was too big to cross the Nantucket bar, but most of her fittings were made on the island.

When school was out and Mother could spare her, Lucretia went with Father to the waterfront workshops. They looked in at the cooper's where men were bending oak staves into barrels. They climbed up into the sail loft to watch a leather-palmed sailmaker push his needle through the *Tryal's* new sails. They visited the blacksmith at his forge and the ropewalk where cordage was spun. Everywhere they walked, Lucretia filled her nostrils with the smell of fish and whale oil, hemp and oak and tar.

On their way home, they stopped at Uncle Rotch's big brick counting house at the foot of Straight Wharf. Father pored over maps and charts while a sailor entertained Lucretia with a squawking parrot that he had brought from the Antilles, or a monkey from Trinidad.

During those afternoons with Father, she caught her first glimpse of the wide world beyond Nantucket Sound. Not everyone on the waterfront was a relative of the Coffins. There were olive-skinned workmen with gold rings through their ears who spoke a strange tongue that her father said was Portuguese. Some of the sailors were Indians, descendants of the original natives of Nantucket. Others were blacks whose fathers had been brought from Africa on slave ships.

The last slaves on Nantucket were set free after the Revolution, but these sailors remained on the island, building homes for their families near Mill Hill. The streets on which they lived had African names—New Guiney, Angola—names that sounded strange to a child who was accustomed to the bluntness of Fair and Main and New Dollar Lane.

Whenever Lucretia was sent to the miller's with corn for grinding, she stared with frank interest at these people with dark skins and tightly curled hair. Once she ventured to talk to a boy and was surprised when he answered her in an accent that was as New England as her own.

"Name's Lucretia Coffin."

"Name's Benjamin Boston."

"Father's Thomas Coffin, a sea captain."

"Father's Prince Boston, a sailor."

"Shipping out next month."

"Mine's been gone 'most a year."

That was all. Lucretia would have liked to continue the conversation, but for once she couldn't think of anything to say. As she trudged up the hill to the windmill, she wondered what it would be like to have a dark skin and parents who had been slaves.

After the *Tryal* set sail from Woods Hole, life went on as it had always done. School and meeting, housework and visitors. Yearly Meeting in May was followed by sheep-shearing in June.

The flocks of sheep that had been grazing on the moors were herded into pens along the edge of Miacomet Pond. After a thorough dousing in the pond to wash away a year-long accumulation of sand and brambles, their wool was clipped. The whole process took three days and all Nantucket turned out to watch and help.

A few hundred yards from the pens, the gray moors were transformed into a carnival town. In flag-decked booths built for the occasion, farmers' wives sold roast pig and three-cornered "shearing buns" and hard-boiled eggs with scarlet shells.

The Coffins camped out in a tent made from old sails, sleeping on quilts on the sandy ground. Lucretia fed bits of her shearing bun to the yearling lambs and watched wide-eyed as the farmers worked over the sheep with their clicking shears. As the wind picked up stray tufts of the creamy-white wool, she raced across the moors with Elizabeth to see who could collect the biggest handful.

In the evenings a fiddler played:

> Tis tu I can't and tu I can
> All the way to shearing-pen

while sailors twirled their girls in reels and fore-and-afters.

Although Friends disapproved of singing and dancing, it was hard to keep from tapping to the measure of the song. Caught up in the excitement, Lucretia joined in.

> *Tis tu I can't—*

Even to her inexperienced ear, it didn't sound right. Breaking off, she looked guiltily at Mother. To her surprise, Anna laughed.

"Thou can't sing even when thou tries," she informed her daughter. "If thou was as far out of town as thou is out of tune, thou wouldn't get home tonight."

In tune or out, Lucretia sometimes felt like singing. The first summer that Father was away, the whole family went to the Folgers' farm. The children fed the chickens and rode the hay wagon and tried mightily to down all the doughnuts that Grandmother piled on their plates.

They spent days picking blueberries on the moors or collecting shells along the beach. Nantucket girls—or any other girls in the first year of the Nineteenth century—didn't swim, but Mother let them take off their shoes and hold up their skirts while they played at the water's edge.

As the gulls cried overhead, Lucretia looked out across the gray Atlantic. Spain, the nearest landfall, was three thousand miles away. It was a big world and she was glad to be part of it.

The world seemed even bigger when Father's first letter arrived with the return address—"Pacific Ocean"—written boldly across the top of the sheet. In the Straits of Magellan he had bought a load of sealskins from Indian hunters. Shipping these furs to Canton on the *Fame*, which was also China-bound, he planned to sail along the Chilean coast in search of a larger cargo.

"It promises to be a long trip," he wrote. "I am hopeful about its outcome, but I fear that thy money will not last until my return. Thou must ask Brother Micajah or Cousin Rotch to help . . ."

Instead of asking for help, Anna cleared the chairs from the small front parlor and converted it into a "Shop of Goods." Traveling to Boston on the packet boat, she traded Nantucket candles and oil for dry goods and groceries. When she returned she stocked her shelves with the pins and needles, tea and spices that her neighbors could not buy on the island.

Mother's shop brought new responsibilities to her daughters. Although Sarah was the oldest, Anna depended increasingly on Lucretia who was quick to understand and quick to carry out all manner of errands. When Anna traveled to the mainland on her trading trips, Lucretia was left in charge of the younger children. Sarah and Elizabeth shared household chores, but it was Lucretia who saw that Mary's dress was properly buttoned and that Thomas's hands were washed before he sat down to supper.

It was Lucretia, too, who organized the games that they played around the fire at night. She picked out the hard words for spelling bees and refereed if there was an argument over jackstraws. When they recited multiplication tables backwards or quoted verses from the Bible she pounced on every mistake.

"Elizabeth," she would scold, "thou has it wrong again. When will thou learn to say it properly?"

Recognizing the echo of her own tone of authority in her daughter's voice, Anna counseled patience. "Thy sister will learn, long tongue. Thou must give her more time."

On evenings when Anna was going to be away, she sometimes allowed the children a special treat. "After you have finished knitting twenty bouts," she told them, "you may go down cellar and pick out as many as you want of the smallest potatoes—the very smallest—and roast them in the ashes."

Potatoes were not everyday fare. When the girls rescued them from the fire with a long-handled fork and ate them in their blackened jackets, they felt as if they were feasting royally.

Another long year went by without any word from Father. Whenever the town crier swung his bell, they stampeded up to the walk. Perhaps it was the *Swallow* or the *Bluebell* or the *Prudence* with a letter. But no letter came.

Mary learned to talk. Thomas was ready for school. Elizabeth grew taller than Lucretia. Life went on, but there were worry lines between Mother's eyes and Lucretia's broad forehead was sometimes creased.

After candles were blown out at night, she and Sarah whispered together in their four-poster bed. Whispered about hurricanes and typhoons, about ships wrecked on hidden shoals, and pirates and privateers. Words that they didn't dare to say aloud in the clear light of day.

As time passed, people began to take it for granted that the *Tryal* was lost and that Father would never return. The aunts were kind. The uncles offered money and advice.

Anna was still calm, but her worry lines deepened and she no longer rushed upstairs when the crier shouted, "Ship's at the bar!"

Then it happened. Not a letter from Father, but Father himself striding down the gangplank when the packet from New Bedford tied up at Straight Wharf!

This time it was a father without a sea chest, without presents for his children—and without the *Tryal*. He bounced Mary on his knee, shook Thomas, Jr., by the hand in proper man-fashion, and hugged his big girls. Lucretia was breathless with excitement as she pushed the chairs in a circle around the hearth.

"*Gracias*," he smiled.

Gracias?

"Spanish for 'thank thee.' No, I haven't been to Spain"—he was answering the question before they asked it—"I've been in Valparaiso, in Chile. But you know that from my letters."

"No letters." Anna shook her head. "No letters for almost two years."

"But I wrote. Whenever I found a ship bound for New England ports. Then you don't know what happened—you must have thought—"

"We—everyone—thought thee lost." Anna's voice trembled.

Father sat in shocked silence. When he spoke his voice was shaky too. "I'm home. And from now on, I'm going to stay in the family circle."

Although his story was a long one, it wasn't as exciting as Lucretia and Sarah had imagined it would be. There were no shipwrecks or pirates. While hunting seals, the *Tryal* had put in at Valparaiso for fresh water and supplies. As soon as she dropped anchor, the Spanish governor ordered her seizure.

"But why? Thou had done no wrong."

"Chile is a Spanish colony and Spain wants to keep it that way," Father explained. "They won't permit the people there to trade with other nations."

"But it's not fair—the governor had no right—"

"Not fair," Father agreed. "But the British and French do the same in their colonies. Politics are not always fair, thou should know."

A stranger in Chile, with no knowledge of the language, Thomas Coffin had fought through the courts for the return of his ship. After more than a year, he gave up the struggle and set out for home. There were months of riding on mule-back through a pass in the Andes and months more before he reached Brazil where he found a whaler on her way back to New Bedford.

The children were fascinated by his description of Valparaiso and by the Spanish words he had learned.

"Tell us again about the mud huts and the men with their big straw hats," Lucretia begged.

"Tomorrow," Mother insisted. "It's far past thy bedtime."

"Buenas noches," Father said.

"Buenas noches," Lucretia answered as she moved slowly toward the stairs.

All that Father had salvaged from the *Tryal* was his strongbox with the ship's log, but he was still hoping to hear from the *Fame*. At last a letter came. His seal skins had fetched $5 a pelt in the Canton market and the *Fame's* skipper was depositing Captain Coffin's share in a Boston bank.

Although there would be money enough for a new ship, Father decided not to go to sea again. He was going to keep the promise he had made on the night of his return. Only . . .

"We shall have to move to Boston. I will go into the mercantile business there."

Leave Nantucket! Lucretia's heart was often heavy in the busy weeks that lay ahead. She and Sarah stayed home from school to help Mother sort and pack the thousand and one things that must be taken along. Barrels were heaped high, boxes nailed closed and sea chests looped with rope.

Finally they were ready. The house on Fair Street had been sold to Aunt Phoebe. On a July day in 1804, Lucretia skipped down its front steps for the last time. From the deck of the Boston packet she waved at the friends who had come to say goodbye—waved until her aching arm could wave no more.

The packet floated over the bar on the incoming tide. As it sailed past the lighthouse on Brant Point, Lucretia ran to the stern. Homes and workshops, sand and moors were slowly blurring. If she shaded her eyes with her hand, she could still see the vanes of the windmills on Mill Hill. After that there was nothing left of Nantucket but a lone seagull silhouetted against the sky.

5. New Ports

*Our teachers are all young, but not lacking their
literary qualifications for the branches they attend
to, and I trust some of them not wholly devoid of a
religious sensibility which qualifies for the moral in-
struction of children. The present price of tuition for
reading, writing and arithmetic is £26 per year,
and with grammar added is £28.*

JAMES MOTT, SR.

Boston in 1804 was half village, half busy city. Herds of cows
still grazed on the Common and there was a whipping post
on State Street. But in the north end of town housewives
were beginning to complain because the black smoke from
Paul Revere's foundry left soot on their clean wash.

The Coffins lived on Green Street in a neighborhood of
well-kept homes and gardens. On First day afternoons,
Lucretia went walking with her father. They stopped to
admire the handsome new houses going up on Bowdoin
Square or crossed the city to see the State House with its
gilded dome where Uncle Micajah Coffin served in the
Massachusetts legislature. Sometimes they visited Long
Wharf to look at the ships from China and distant Russia
that were waiting to unload cargoes there. From his office on
the wharf, Thomas Coffin bought and sold all manner of
goods—silks and carpets and even bananas, the sweet-tast-
ing fruit that a sea captain introduced to Boston that year.

As they wandered along the narrow cobblestoned streets,
little Lucretia gawked at the elegant carriages and their

occupants. There were ladies in brocaded gowns and men wearing velvet-collared coats and pantaloons. Pantaloons—long trousers—were a new fashion imported from France. When President Jefferson wore them at his inauguration, his enemies called them "undemocratic"!

The change from Quaker Nantucket to worldly Boston was an abrupt one, and the Coffins worried about its effect on their children. At first they attended private school, along with the daughters and sons of other well-to-do-merchants. But Thomas, fearing that the select school was "ministering to a feeling of class pride," soon transferred them to a Free School near their home where, he said, they could "mingle with all classes without distinction."

Boston was one of the few American cities with a public school system, its Reading and Writing schools promising "equal equality" for all. At the Free School, Lucretia met girls poorer than herself and learned something of the lives of the city's struggling artisans—but she learned little else.

For "equal equality" did not apply to girls. Boys went to school year-round, girls only in the slow summer session from April to October. Boys studied Latin and Greek and dreamed of going to Harvard College some day. Girls knew quite enough, their elders said, when they could sew a shirt, bake a pudding, and write their names.

Thomas, son of a schoolmaster, wanted more than this for his daughters. Fifteen-year-old Sarah was clearly not cut out to be a scholar, but a better school would have to be found for Lucretia and Elizabeth. After corresponding with Friends in other towns, he decided to send them to a Quaker boarding school at Nine Partners, New York.

Nine Partners was a crossroads settlement, fifteen miles from Poughkeepsie, in the valley of the Hudson River. From Green Street in Boston it sounded like the wild West. The

journey there was so long and costly that the girls would
not be able to return home for two years.

"Two whole years!" Elizabeth groaned.

"It's like a trip to China," Lucretia tried to comfort her.

Preparing for Nine Partners was almost like getting ready
for a China voyage. For weeks Anna and her daughters
shopped and sewed. The school had sent a list of the "strong
and substantial clothing" that they must bring:

       1 or 2 plain bonnets
       1 cloak (not silk)
       2 or 3 plain short gowns
       3 night caps
       3 or 4 pair of yarn stockings
       3 gingham dark neck handkerchiefs
       4 shifts
       3 long check aprons
       1 pair of scissors and a paper of pins
       Comb and brush, pen knife
       Pieces of cloth, thread and yarn for mending

"If the clothing sent be not plain or require much washing, it is to be returned or colored at the parents' expense,"
the head teacher warned.

At dawn on a spring morning in 1806, the driver of the
New York Mail Stage lashed their horsehair trunk to the
top of his coach. Thomas boosted his daughters up the high
step and climbed aboard after them. The driver gathered
his reins in his hands, clucked to his horses, and they were
off!

Lucretia and Elizabeth sat side by side on the front bench.
Leather curtains covered three sides of the stage but if they
looked straight ahead over the backs of the horses, they
could see the familiar farms and stony pastures of New
England. As the stage jogged along, covering three or four
miles an hour, the girls began to enjoy themselves. They ate

the lunch that Anna had packed for them, talked to fellow passengers, and climbed down to stretch their legs whenever the driver stopped to deliver mail. At night they slept in a tavern by the side of the road, sharing a room with other lady passengers. By the time they reached New York, three dusty days later, they felt like seasoned travelers.

After a bath and a night's rest at the home of a Friend, the Albany stage carried them up the Hudson. They drove through towns with tongue-twisting Dutch names and past broad fields of wheat and corn. Occasionally the road turned inland through dark forests where there was no sign of human life. Then the passengers talked of bears and wildcats and the bounty paid for the heads of wolves—and even Lucretia reached for Father's hand. After another night at an inn, the stagecoach rattled on, rumbling over the planks of covered bridges, skirting river and forest, until it reached Poughkeepsie.

For the last lap of the journey, the horsehair trunk was loaded into a private carriage. Lucretia perched on the edge of her seat, eager to catch every detail of her new home. The neighborhood wasn't as wild as she had expected it to be. Pioneers, mostly Friends from New England and Long Island, had built sawmills on the streams and cleared the woods for farming. As they approached the school, they passed shops—a blacksmith, a shoemaker, a silversmith—and a brick meeting house larger than the one in Boston.

The carriage wheels squeaked to a stop in front of a building that looked like an outsize barn. The schoolhouse which had once been a store was three stories high and almost a hundred feet long, with two sets of front steps and two front doors. The mystery of the two entrances was soon explained. One half of the long house was for boys, the other for girls, with a parlor in between where brothers and sisters might meet on First days. Even the playground was divided by a high board fence over which close relatives—and only close relatives—were permitted to speak "under suitable inspection at proper seasons."

Nine Partners' rules for its students covered everything from "proper books" to "improper familiarity" between boys and girls. Anna Coffin's daughters found little difficulty in adjusting to a routine of early-to-rise and early-to-bed. They "preserved a commendable decorum" in classes, walked to meeting house "in an orderly and becoming manner" and kept their clothing "in good order and repair."

In spite of its strict regulations, the school was liberal in comparison with other schools where teachers kept order with a willow switch. Friends believed in reasoning with the children instead of whipping them and the teachers were expected to act as "parents and directors of a well-ordered family."

Even in the best-ordered family there are times when rules are broken and children rebel against authority. Lucretia had only been at Nine Partners for a short while when she learned that a boy had been sentenced to a day in a dark closet with a bread and water diet. Convinced that his punishment was unfair, she took justice in her own hands. Leading an expedition into the boys' side of the school, she comforted the prisoner in the best way she knew—by sliding slices of buttered bread under the closet door.

While shy Elizabeth remained on the sidelines, Lucretia quickly became a leader. One of the girls' favorite after-school games was "meeting." Imitating their parents' monthly business meetings, they acted out instances of Friends who had violated Quaker discipline. As soon as Lucretia's talents as a mimic were discovered she was given the part of an elder to play.

"Friends," she would report in her best copy of a grownup voice, "we have visited Tabitha Field—and we labored with her—and we think we mellowed her some."

Thirteen was an age for best friends and Lucretia found one in Sarah Mott, a girl a year older than she. It wasn't long before they slept in adjoining beds in the big dormitory room and whispered confidences after "Candles out!" each night. As the spring days lengthened into summer they spent their free hours playing battledore and shuttlecock, or hiking over the hills for a view of the Hudson.

When winter snows made hiking difficult for girls with ankle-length skirts, they tramped through the drifts behind the school to a tiny playhouse. There they baked biscuits and cake and sometimes were allowed to give a tea party for the boys—"under suitable inspection," of course.

There were almost as many Motts at Nine Partners as there were Coffins on Nantucket. Lucretia and Sarah counted sisters Mary and Abby, cousins Arthur and Alfred, Aunt Lydia who taught the girls' sewing classes . . .

"James Mott," Lucretia continued.

"Two James Motts," Sarah corrected her. "Grandfather James and brother James."

Lucretia had caught glimpses of Sarah's brother over the playground fence. Indeed, it was hard not to notice him because at eighteen he was the tallest boy in the school, with blue eyes and a shock of sandy hair. Grandfather James, his dignified elderly namesake, was a founder of Nine Partners. As a member of its supervising committee, he spent most of his time at the school.

During the school's two-week vacation, Lucretia went home with Sarah and met more Motts—Sarah's parents, Adam and Anne, her younger brother, Richard, and an assortment of uncles and aunts. The Motts lived on adjoining farms in Mamaroneck, some twenty miles from New York City, operating a family flour mill on the rocky shore of Long Island Sound.

All of the older Motts were active in Friends' concerns, serving as clerks of their meetings and traveling to the northern outposts of the state to visit Indian settlements. In their presence, Lucretia felt more than a twinge of homesickness. Her last letter from Boston had told of the birth of a baby sister. Little Martha—"who looks like thee" Mother had written—would be half-grown before they even met!

Sarah's family did their best to make Lucretia feel at home. Although bashful James was too shy to talk much to girls, he took them sailing on the mill pond and drove them along the country road in his father's phaeton. In the evenings, the young people crowded into the kitchen where Jinny and Billy, the family's servants, entertained them.

Jinny, a former slave, told tales of her African childhood— "summer all the time, no ice, no snow"—while Billy strummed on a homemade banjo. When it was his turn to talk, he puffed on a stubby pipe—"better than a long one for keeping my nose warm"—and talked about Revolutionary times when he had hidden whaleboatmen from the British in the inlets near the mill. Even after the hickory logs had burned to embers there was always one more song, one more story that "Lucretia must hear."

6. School Days

*My sympathy was early enlisted for the poor slave
by the class-books read in our school. The unequal
condition of woman with man also early impressed
my mind.*

LUCRETIA MOTT

In her second year at school, Lucretia moved into the class
with the oldest girls to study Grammar, Literature, Math-
ematics, and Geography. The principal teacher, Susan
Marriott, was an English woman who drilled and scolded,
pleading with her pupils to learn the fine points of grammar
and exact word meanings.

"No, no Lucretia," she would say. "Thou must see the
difference between 'distrust' and 'mistrust.' Be precise."

Novels were frowned on and even Shakespeare and romantic poets like Wordsworth and Coleridge were not on
Quaker reading lists. Instead, the girls memorized long passages from eighteenth-century authors whose verses carried a moral. Lucretia's favorite was William Cowper. When,
with flashing eyes and ringing voice, she recited:

> "I would not have a slave to till my ground,
> To carry me, to fan me while I sleep,
> And tremble when I wake, for all the gold
> That sinews bought and sold have ever earned.
> No; dear as freedom is, and in my heart's
> Just estimation, prized above all price,
> I would much rather be myself the slave,
> And wear the bonds, than fasten them on him."

even Susan Marriott said, "Well spoken."

Slavery was a refrain that ran through Lucretia's days at Nine Partners. On Nantucket it had belonged to a remote past. At Nine Partners it suddenly became real. For the men and women who plowed the Dutch farms nearby were not freedmen, like the families on New Guiney Street. They were slaves, bound by New York State law to serve their masters for another twenty years.

Only two pictures adorned the classroom walls. One showed William Penn signing a peace treaty with the Indians. The other was a drawing of a slave ship, showing the kidnaped Africans stacked in the hold like so many pieces of stove wood. The school reader—titled *Mental Inprovement or the Beauties and Wonders of Instructive Conversation* —printed the same picture, along with a description of the slave trade that Thomas Clarkson, an English abolitionist, had written. At the end of Clarkson's report, the reader commented, "Humanity shudders at your account!"

But slavery was not the only topic of conversation at Nine Partners in 1807. One crisp fall day, the older pupils crowded into a farm wagon and drove to Poughkeepsie. Standing on a bluff overlooking the Hudson, they watched a strange sail-less craft make its way upriver. Its paddle wheels splashed and dark clouds billowed from its smoke stack as it traveled on to Albany.

The voyage of the *Clermont* was soon overshadowed by Jefferson's embargo, which forbade American ships to sail to foreign ports. The embargo was intended as a peace measure, to keep the United States out of the war in which England and France were engaged. Its immediate effect, however, was to throw thousands out of work in New England and New York.

"Thou cannot imagine the desolation here," Anna wrote Lucretia. "Sailors, mates and even masters line up at soup

kitchens for food and the prisons are overflowing with debt-
ors. Thy father is still doing business with coastwise vessels,
but I fear he must soon cast about for other means of livelihood." She had copied out a rhyme from a local newspaper:

> Our ships all in motion once whitened the ocean,
> They sailed and returned with a cargo.
> Now doomed to decay, they have fallen a prey
> To Jefferson—worms—and embargo.

Almost everyone at Nine Partners was receiving similar
letters from home. When Lucretia hunted up Sarah she
found her in tears. Most of the flour ground at the Mott's
mill had formerly been shipped to France. With this market
cut off, the mill was in danger of failing. Sarah's parents were
obliged to move from their farm to smaller quarters in the
mill house.

"And," Sarah mourned, "they say we must come home
from school."

Of all the Mott tribe, only the two Jameses were to remain
at Nine Partners. James Senior would become Superintend-
ent of the school while his grandson taught the younger boys.

The first months after Sarah left were lonely ones for
Lucretia. No one else in the school quite filled her place.
When two new pupils arrived she welcomed them. They
were Elizabeth and Sarah Hicks, daughters of Elias Hicks,
a well-known Quaker preacher.

Lucretia had never seen anyone like Hicks before. He was
a dynamic speaker with piercing black eyes and a resonant
voice. She sat in rapt attention when he talked in meeting.

As a member of the school committee, Hicks stayed at
Nine Partners for a few weeks to assist Grandfather Mott.
One morning he visited the girls' geography class. Twirling
the globe on her desk, their teacher silently begged her pupils to be models of wisdom and deportment.

They were studying South America. "Chimborazo," she said. "Who can tell us about Chimborazo? Thou, Lucretia—"

Conscious of the distinguished visitor in the back of the room, Lucretia rose to recite. The famous explorer, Baron Alexander von Humboldt, had recently climbed Mount Chimborazo. Besides, she was brimming over with information from her father's South American trip.

"Chimborazo is a volcano in the Andes. It's 12,500 feet high and it's covered with snow and—" The facts were spilling out when a snort interrupted her.

"A waste of time," Elias Hicks declared. "A sheer waste of time to teach girls the height of mountains. Teach them something that will be useful to them in after life."

Lucretia's cheeks grew hot and she bit her lip to keep back an answer. Boston said things like that, but not Nine Partners! Although she continued to admire Hicks as a preacher and thinker, she never quite forgave him.

Her second year at school was drawing to a close when Grandfather Mott stopped her in the corridor. "How would thou like to teach next year?" he asked.

Lucretia didn't know what to answer. She had been looking forward to home, to seeing Mother and Father, brother and sisters again. Little Martha whom she had never seen would be celebrating her second birthday soon. Still, to be a real teacher . . .

"Thou would assist Deborah Rogers, teaching reading, writing, and arithmetic," he continued. "No salary beyond room and board, but thou could keep on with thy studies as well. If thou likes, I will write thy parents."

While Elizabeth returned to Boston, Lucretia moved her belongings from the girls' dormitory to a bedroon next to Deborah's. Suddenly she was grown up, with all of the privileges and responsibilities that went with her new position.

No more mischief, no more rebellion now that she was on the other side of the teacher's desk!

Young James Mott smiled as he watched her bustle into the teachers' sitting room with a load of books under her arm. Even with her bonnet on—the bonnet that she tied with extra care these days—she scarcely came to his shoulder.

"Thou looks younger than thy pupils," he said.

"I'll be sixteen soon," Lucretia bristled, "and as for thee, James Mott—" She stopped when she saw that he was blushing to the roots of his flaxen hair. It was hard to stay angry with this tall young man who was so tongue-tied and unsure of himself.

As the months sped by, she found herself spending more and more time with Sarah's big bashful brother. Together they organized a French class for the teachers. After supper on winter evenings they sat before the fire struggling with declensions and a unfamiliar vocabulary. When spring came, he took Sarah's place as her companion outdoors. As they walked through the woods hunting for the first creamy-white hepaticas, he hesitantly unburdened himself.

"Thou cannot imagine how much I dislike teaching, how unequal I feel to the task."

"If I were thee, I should leave," Lucretia promptly counseled. "Thou could find another position."

"That's not easy now." James shook his head. "Even my hundred pounds a year is useful to my parents."

Lucretia pricked up her ears. "How much did thou say thou earned, James?"

"One hundred pounds a year. No great sum, but—"

Lucretia frowned. Without another word, she turned back toward the school. James hurried to keep step with her.

"Deborah," she called when she reached the sitting room.

"Didn't thou say that thy salary was forty pounds a year?"
Deborah nodded.

"Sarah?" Lucretia turned to Sarah Southwick, another
teacher.

"Twenty pounds. But of course I'm new this year."

"Caleb?"

The boys' head teacher looked up from the book he was
reading. "One hundred and twenty pounds."

Lucretia's eyes grew dangerously dark. "I suppose the
boys pay more for tuition than the girls?"

"Both pay the same. Thou know that, Lucretia," James
answered.

"But—but—" Lucretia sputtered, falling back on the language of childhood. "It's not fair. Deborah has been
a teacher longer than thou. Because thou art a man, thy pay
is more than double hers."

Feeling as if he were a prisoner at the bar, James stared
at the polished pine floor. If it would please Lucretia, he
would gladly turn over his salary to Deborah.

"Oh, it's not thy fault." Lucretia reached up to pat his
sagging shoulder.

The discussion ended, but the incident was another of
those to be filed away and not forgotten. "The injustice of
the distinction was so apparent," she later wrote, "that I
resolved to claim for my sex all that an impartial Creator
had bestowed."

At the end of the term, when Lucretia was asked to remain at Nine Partners as a salaried teacher, she decided
against it. Boarding school days were over and it was time
to go home.

Home was no longer in Boston. The embargo had finally
driven Captain Coffin from the waterfront—but it had also
provided him with a new livelihood. When trade with

Europe was cut off, Americans began to manufacture many kinds of goods that they had previously imported. After Thomas Coffin sold his commission business on Long Wharf, he invested the proceeds in a factory that was making cut nails.

"Cut nails?" Lucretia was puzzled when she first heard the word.

"Nails used in building," James explained. "Several nail factories are starting up in Pennsylvania."

"That's where Father's is." Lucretia nodded. "In French Creek, about twenty miles from Philadelphia. They—we— are moving there."

To James, Philadelphia sounded as far away as the moon. "I'll miss thee, Lucretia," he stammered.

Lucretia tilted back her head to look into his face. Solid, serious, slow James was beginning to mean a great deal to her. She could run rings around him in a conversation, but he had a rock-like quality that came from more than his size.

"I'll miss thee, too, James Mott," she softly answered.

7. I Take Thee, James

Lucretia and myself declared our intentions of marriage on Fourth-day last. Our appearance was plain, and becoming the occasion. All parties were pleased with it.

JAMES MOTT

Anna Coffin caught her breath as Lucretia stepped from the deck of the Camden ferryboat. The little girl who had waved goodbye in Boston three years earlier was a young woman now. A trim figure in dove gray, with bonnet and cap hiding her long brown hair, she was almost beautiful. But fashion decreed that ladies should be pale and languid, and Lucretia's chin was too firm, her forehead too high and her fine dark eyes too bright and knowing. Even her walk was wrong. Instead of taking mincing, dainty steps, she strode across the gangplank with a clatter of heel and toe that announced strength and determination.

Brother and sisters crowded around, but little Martha claimed her attention first. Tugging at Lucretia's hand, she proudly led the way home. The Coffins lived on Second Street, in a red brick house with white shutters and white marble steps. It was the twin of every other house on the street. The sidewalk out front was paved with brick; in the back there was a narrow yard with a patch of lawn and a charcoal furnace where meals were cooked in summer.

Before Lucretia could take off her shawl a chorus of voices insisted on her presence in the kitchen.

"We have a surprise for thee," eleven-year-old Thomas announced.

"A pump, a pump!" Jumping up and down in excitement, Martha gave the surprise away.

In the kitchen, Thomas raised and lowered the pump handle until a stream of water splashed into the sink. Philadelphia was the first city in the United States to have its own waterworks. Using steam power, water was carried from the Schuylkill River to a reservoir in Centre Square. From there it traveled through hollowed pine logs to the city's homes and shops.

"Taste it." Sarah filled a glass. "It's good."

"Mighty cold in winter." Elizabeth pretended to shiver. "Wish somebody would think of a way to heat it."

Thomas who was at the tinkering stage looked thoughtful. "Maybe I will. Maybe I'll invent something."

"Oh, pshaw." Mary nudged him with her elbow. "None of thy inventions ever work."

Lucretia laughed, wishing she could hug all of them at once. How had she managed to stay away so long from her noisy, lively, loving family?

She liked Philadelphia immediately. The largest city in the land, it still reflected its Quaker founder, William Penn. Where Boston had twisting lanes and narrow alleys, Philadelphia's streets were laid out in checkerboard fashion, with a geometrical precision that she approved of. Penn had even named them Quaker style, with Second Street followed by Third, Fourth by Fifth, and so on. The intersecting avenues were named after local trees and flowers.

> "High, Mulberry, Sassafrass, Vine,
> Chestnut, Walnut, Spruce and Pine"

Martha recited the jingle for her.

Penn's City of Brotherly Love had grown into a metropolis under the influence of Benjamin Franklin. More than any other man, he was responsible for the city's modernity—for its clean paved streets, its whale-oil street lamps, its hospital, library, police and fire companies. Even the stove that the Coffins used for heating their parlor had been invented by Cousin Benjamin.

After the quiet of Nine Partners, Lucretia was captivated by the city's noise and bustle. From early morning until late at night, there was always something happening on Second Street. The baker delivered bread in a handcart. The milkman measured out his milk in bright tins at each front door. The fisherwoman walked by with a tray on her head, calling "You buy an-y sha-a-d? Any perch? Any catfeesh?" They were followed by the pepperpot woman, the hominy man, the bean-soup woman. And the hot-muffin man, the molasses-candy woman, the ice-cream man.

After dark a watchman made his rounds. Lantern in hand, he paused at the corner to call the hours. "Ten o'clock and all's well . . . Twelve o'clock and a rainy night . . . Past three o'clock and frosty morning . . ." It was comforting to lie in bed and listen.

In winter, a wood-splitter, ax at shoulder and wedges jingling on a string, marched down the sidewalk. In spring, there were crews with pails and brushes singing, "Here's the white, white-wash! Brown white-wash! Yellow whitewash! Green whitey-wash! We're about!" In summer, the charcoal man blew on his horn, calling "Charco, charco!"

Lucretia had often helped her mother make soap from ashes and kitchen fat. Now a man bought their leftover ashes and fat, selling it back to them as "soft soap" a few days later. There was even a sandman who sold sand by the quart so that housewives could scour their sooty pots.

"Buying sand!" The girl from Nantucket shook her head reproachfully.

Anna was amused. "We're in the city now, Lucretia. Thou'll have to get used to new ways."

As an outlet for his factory at French Creek, Thomas Coffin had opened a store on Dock Street, a few squares from home. Sales of cut nails were going so well that he considered adding other merchandise to his stock.

"Won't thou need a clerk to assist thee?" Lucretia blurted out the question as her father showed her through the store one afternoon.

"If business continues well, I'm thinking of engaging a young man." Father nodded. "But why does thou ask?"

"It's just that—I thought perhaps—"

Father's eyebrows lifted. It wasn't often that talkative Lucretia stuttered and stammered. "Thou thought perhaps that there might be an opening for thy friend, James Mott?"

Lucretia reddened. "He would be good and steady. And he is so unhappy at his teaching position. And—"

"And thou? Art thou unhappy?"

"Not unhappy, but—I miss him," she confessed.

Thomas Coffin took a deep breath. "Thy mother and I have not been unaware of thy feelings. The Motts are well thought of among New York Friends. Thy young man—I cannot promise anything now, but in a few months' time, perhaps."

For optimistic Lucretia, her father's "perhaps" was almost as good as a promise. She flew home to write to James. The months became weeks, the weeks, days, and at last it was settled. James was to come to Philadelphia to work in Father's store.

"James is coming. James is coming." She wove the words into a secret little song, humming it to herself when she was sure that no one was listening.

As the day of arrival drew near, she threw herself into

a round of feverish activity. James must taste her blackberry pudding . . . James must admire her new dress . . . Would he mind sharing a room with Thomas, Jr.? Would he approve of the parlor chairs?

"What's the matter with thee?" her brother grumbled. "Thou cleaned my wardrobe three times today."

"Yesterday she scrubbed the front steps in the morning and again in the afternoon. The very same steps." Mary snickered.

Sarah and Elizabeth exchanged amused glances. "Lucretia," Sarah said, "thou acts the way Mother used to when Father's ship was sailing around Brant Point. Dost thou remember?"

"Except that Mother didn't spend so long in front of the mirror trying different ways of tying her cap," Elizabeth pointed out.

Lucretia reddened and refused to answer their teasing. She had more important things on her mind. It had been a whole year since she left Nine Partners. Had James changed? What would he be like?

When James arrived he was exactly as he had always been, a little taller perhaps and a little less shy. He liked the blackberry pudding, the parlor chairs, the third-floor bedroom—and he plainly liked Lucretia.

Happy, she introduced him to the city that she had adopted as her own. On Chestnut Street they wandered through the State House where, thirty-four years earlier, the Declaration of Independence had been signed. It was a museum now, its upstairs rooms crowded with stuffed birds and mastodon bones. There were Indians squatting on the grass in front of the State House. They stopped to watch the men shooting at pennies with bows and arrows while the women peddled moccasins and straw baskets.

But this was old Philadelphia. On their way home they passed the new marble bank buildings that everyone was talking about. The Bank of Pennsylvania on Second Street was a copy of a temple in Greece.

"There's no building in the country that can rival it," Lucretia informed James with what could only be called civic pride.

He smiled. "Thou has become a true Philadelphian."

"And thou?" she anxiously asked. "Dost thou think thou will like it here?"

His face clouded over. "The question is, will Philadelphia like me? Thy father's business is so different from teaching. Suppose I fail?"

"James Mott," Lucretia scolded. "Thou must stop thy eternal worrying. Thou has a good head on thy shoulders and all thou has to do is use it."

Although James was still filled with self-doubt when he entered Thomas Coffin's store, he soon found that Lucretia was right. If you were quick with figures and cheerful with customers, storekeeping was less taxing than teaching. After he had been in Philadelphia for six months, Thomas Coffin offered him a partnership and a third share of the profits.

"A very noble offer," James wrote to his mother and father. "My yearly income promises to be over $2000, but even if it should only be $1500 I would be satisfied."

The "noble offer" meant more than business success. During the months of his apprenticeship, he and Lucretia had come to an understanding. After both the Coffins and Motts consented, they went before a committe of Friends to be questioned on their "clearness for proceeding in marriage."

Once they had "passed meeting," every post carried invitations to the wedding and every post brought acceptances. The date was set for the 10th of Fourth Month, 1811.

Dressed in gray except for her crisp white cap and kerchief, Lucretia sat next to James on the elders bench of the Pine Street meeting house. James, stiff in his new broadcloth suit, gave her a sidelong glance of sympathy.

There was no bridal veil or bouquet, no wedding march, no minister to read the ceremony. According to Quaker custom, the young couple rose, hand in hand, and faced each other.

"In the presence of the Lord and this assembly I take thee, Lucretia Coffin, to be my wife, promising with divine assistance to be unto thee a loving and faithful husband until death shall separate us," James said.

Lucretia, shining-eyed, repeated the words. "I take thee, James Mott, to be my husband . . ."

After they sat down, two ushers brought them a table with a piece of parchment on it. It was their marriage certificate. Lucretia signed her new name for the first time, writing "*Lucretia C. Mott*" in big bold letters.

The solemn ceremony was followed by a gay reception at the Coffins. Almost two hundred people crowded around to add their names to the marriage certificate and to wish the young couple a long happy life together. As Folgers and Macys from Nantucket met Motts from Mamaroneck and New York, little Martha skipped through the crowd asking in her high-pitched little girl's voice, "Is this a wedding?"

8. Hard Times

*These trials in early life were not without their good
effect in disciplining the mind, and leading it to set
a just estimate on worldly pleasures.*

LUCRETIA MOTT

In the neat new home that they rented on Union Street,
Lucretia played at keeping house for James. She stitched
tablecloths and hemmed sheets and scoured the market for
interesting foods to prepare.

The big roofed-over market on High Street was a far
cry from Nantucket. Almost any morning, Lucretia had a
choice of turkey and chicken—and opossum, bear, or bright-
plumaged wild fowl from the woods. Wagoners drove in
from Pittsburgh and beyond loaded to their wheel hubs
with wheat and corn and pork. Farmers from Chester and
Bucks County brought their beef and mutton to the city on
the hoof, decorating prize animals with ribbons and flowers
and hiring trumpeters to advertise their wares.

Shy James was easy to please. He would have eaten un-
derdone meat and scorched biscuits without complaint if
Lucretia had served them. Only once in those first months
did they come close to quarreling. Lucretia was still exasperated when she told the story to her mother. Following
Nantucket custom, she never served butter at the dinner
table. Week after week, James had eaten dry bread with
his meal without comment.

"Then yesterday I absent-mindedly set the butter dish out.
Can thou imagine what he said? 'I'm so glad thou has given

us butter. We always had it for dinner at home.' Never a word before then! What can I do with a man like that?"

"Cherish him," Anna drily advised.

Lucretia did. But her carefree honeymoon days did not last for long. The United States, which had doubled in size since her birth, was troubled by growing pains at home and new threats of war from abroad. The Motts had been married only a year when the threat of war became a reality.

Along the Atlantic coast where prosperity depended on shipping, Mr. Madison's War (as the War of 1812 was called) was roundly denounced. The British fleet anchored off Cape May, bottling up Philadelphia's harbor. Any ships that dared to put to sea were captured and scuttled.

"Business is very dull," James was soon writing to Mamaroneck. "Many failures have taken place and no doubt many more will. All confidence is destroyed and those who have money keep it in their own hands."

The firm of Coffin and Mott managed to stay open but it could barely support two families. To cut down on expenses, the Coffins gave up their Second Street home and moved in with Lucretia and James. "The house is sufficiently large to accommodate us all and leave one spare chamber," James told his parents.

The spare room did not remain empty for long. In the summer of 1812, just before the U.S. *Constitution* captured the British vessel *Guerrière* in America's first naval victory of the war, Lucretia gave birth to a daughter, Anna.

Now she could no longer play at housekeeping. With a baby to care for and less money to spend, she hunted for bargains instead of delicacies on High Street. There were few bargains to be had. Speculators were buying up supplies from the farmers and driving the prices of bread and meat sky-high. For the first time Lucretia saw hunger and hopelessness on people's faces.

Even the street noises had a different sound. A country woman with a shawl over her head went from door to door begging:

"You that have money—and I have got none—
Come buy my hot sweet corn, and let me be gone."

There was a pleading note in the "Sweep oh!" of the chimney sweep and in the oysterman's mournful chant, "Oys! Poor Jack wants his money for selling pickled oysters!"

Only the jingling bells on the teams of horses pulling Conestoga wagons sounded cheerful. Every day more and more of these big wagons with their billowing canvas tops drove through the streets on their way to the West. With business in the city at a standstill, Philadelphians were catching "Ohio fever." James threatened to come down with it too when Mayhew Folger, Anna Coffin's brother, arrived in the city.

Uncle Mayhew had made international news a few years earlier when his whaler, the *Topaz*, put in at Pitcairn Island and there discovered the last of the mutineers from H.M.S. *Bounty*. Now that the war was driving whaleboats from the sea, the veteran skipper had decided to trade the *Topaz* for a prairie schooner.

James and Lucretia seriously considered going to Ohio with Uncle Mayhew. The only thing holding them back was the fact that Lucretia was pregnant again and James was afraid that the trip across the Alleghenies would prove too hard for her. They were still debating the move when a letter came from Uncle Richard Mott offering James a position in his cotton mill in Mamaroneck.

Anna was a talkative twenty-month old when her parents

arrived at the Motts' mill house on Long Island Sound. Her brother Thomas was born three months later. Their stay in Mamaroneck was a pleasant interlude for Lucretia. While Anna played along the shore of the mill pond and Thomas napped in his cradle on the porch, she enjoyed a reunion with James's sisters.

Although the young women found much to gossip about, the war was never far from their thoughts. Two British frigates were anchored in the Sound, in full view of the mill house. Old Billy, who was still working for the Motts, shook his head in disgust when he took Anna for a walk up the beach.

"Them fellows ought to be drove off," he said.

But the frigates stayed and the war continued. Business conditions in Mamaroneck were little better than they had been in Pennsylvania. As the summer drew to a close, James ruefully decided to return to Philadelphia. They were preparing for the journey when word came of the fall of Washington. British troops had set fire to the Capitol and White House and forced the President and Mrs. Madison to flee. Now the enemy was heading toward Philadelphia!

Worry over the fate of her parents strengthened Lucretia's conviction that war, under any circumstances, was wrong. In the anxious days that followed, she spent all of her free hours helping Uncle Richard stitch together peace almanacs—calendars decorated with anti-war sentiments—which he gave to neighbors and friends. Sixty years—and two wars—later, she still remembered his efforts to bring "this cruel war" to an end.

Lacking a telegraph or radio, it was many weeks before the Motts learned that the British had been stopped at Baltimore and, at almost the same moment, defeated on Lake

Champlain. As soon as they were sure that the tide of war had turned, they set out for Philadelphia.

In the fall of 1814, the trip was "quite as comfortable as we could expect," Lucretia wrote to Anne Mott. "We found the roads pretty good till we got to Brunswick, where we dined. From there to Trenton they were exceedingly rough, large stones having been laid where the holes used to be. We were obliged to keep little Thomas well wedged in, that he need not be thrown against the side of the stage. He was very quiet, slept most of the day and was not out of the stage, except when we stopped to dine, until we arrived at Trenton at half-past seven. He was then put to bed and slept quietly all night. The steamboat was quite a relief and we reached Philadelphia at 12 o'clock the next day."

While British and American diplomats dickered over the terms of a peace treaty, James found work in a wholesale plow store. His salary of $600 promised only a scant living for his family—"all we can expect in the unsettled state of affairs and all we ought to be anxious for," he said. The Motts were settling down to the routine of Philadephia living again when, without warning, disaster struck.

Thomas Coffin died of typhus fever. Husband, father, friend was gone and with him the last shred of financial security for the household on Union Street. Shortly before his death he had endorsed a note for a friend. When the friend's business failed, Thomas's property had to be sold to meet the note. James, who still owned a third of the Dock Street store, found that he owned a third of a mountain of debts.

"I feel a responsibility unknown before," he confided to his parents. Even optimistic Lucretia wrote, "Our late irreparable loss has altered the face of all our prospects so that at times everything I look toward appears dark and gloomy."

In the crisis, Anna Coffin came to the fore. Still vigorous at fifty-three, she refused to accept help from James, or from Benjamin Yarnall, her daughter Elizabeth's husband. Within days after Thomas's death, she made plans for a shop similar to the one she had kept on Nantucket. Women shopkeepers were a rarity in Philadelphia but to everyone's surprise, her enterprise proved successful.

James and Lucretia soon followed her example. Renting a store on Fourth Street near the center of the city, they stocked it with goods. Each morning James opened the shutters hopefully. Each night he slowly closed them. Few customers came and in less than a year they were obliged to sell out at a loss.

With the failure of one business venture after another, James's small supply of self-confidence oozed away. "James is discouraged," Lucretia reported again and again. "James is down cellar lately. Though he is acknowledged to be head and shoulders above his brethren, yet he is often complaining of his littleness and leanness."

For six lonely months James tried his luck in New York, working as a clerk in a bank on Wall Street. Even when he returned home to a position as bookkeeper in a friend's store, he felt insecure. To lift some of the burden from his shoulders, Lucretia decided to go to work. In the spring of 1817, she and her cousin, Rebecca Bunker, opened a Select School for Girls, which was sponsored by the Friends Pine Street Meeting.

Starting with four girls who paid $7 a quarter for lessons, the school grew rapidly. Before the end of the year, the two young women were teaching reading, writing, ciphering, and even French, to forty pupils.

The school was several miles from home and there was no public transportation in the city. Philadelphians traveled by private carriage or on foot. Lucretia walked, sharing a cold dinner with Rebecca between the morning and afternoon sessions.

It was dusk before she returned to Union Street, but she was grateful for the long day, glad to be so tired at night that she tumbled into bed without thinking. For only weeks before her first classes started, she received a blow that was all but crushing. Little Thomas—her active, fat, rosy-cheeked two-year old—was dead. He had been stricken by a mysterious fever. In those days of poor sanitation and old-fashioned medicine, there was scarcely a household in the country that had not faced similar tragedy. But this made it no easier for Lucretia to bear.

She continued to teach, leaving the school in 1818 six weeks before a second daughter, Maria, was born. By then James's salary as a bookkeeper had been increased to $1000 a year.

They were still far from rich. Even so small an item as postage on the frequent letters to James's parents had to be reckoned in their budget. A letter to Mamaroneck cost 12½ cents for a single page of correspondence, with the fee paid either by the sender or the recipient. To save this money, they were in the habit of sending their letters in the care of friends traveling to New York. In the spring of 1819, eight years after their marriage, James at last felt that he was on his feet. He wrote exultantly to his father, "Answer this letter by *mail*. The expense is trifling, now that I have money of my *own* to pay it!"

9. The Growing-up Years

*I have had six children. Not accustomed to resign-
ing them to the care of a nurse, I was much confined to them during their infancy and childhood.
Being fond of reading, I omitted much unnecessary
stitching and ornamental work in the sewing for my
family so that I might have more time for the improvement of the mind.*

LUCRETIA MOTT

Throughout the 1820s there was always a baby in the
cradle and two or three toddlers racing through the Motts'
house. A second Thomas was born in 1823, followed by
Elizabeth two years later. Martha, who was nicknamed
Patty to distinguish her from her Aunt Martha, was born
in 1828.

As his family increased, James's income kept pace with it.
Leaving his bookkeeper's job, he went into business for himself as a cotton commission merchant. By 1824, he was able
to move from Anna Coffin's and rent a comfortable house
on Sansom Street.

After the Motts left, Anna Coffin gave up her shop and
filled her empty rooms with lodgers. Her rooms soon
seemed empty indeed, for in the space of one year her
daughters, Sarah and Mary, died and Martha married an
Army captain and moved to the Territory of Florida. Not
long afterward, Martha's young husband was killed and
she returned to Philadelphia with an infant daughter, Mariana, to care for.

In the closeknit Coffin clan, one person's troubles were

shouldered by all. Lucretia had already taken in Sister
Mary's baby, Anna Temple. Now she opened her door to
little Mariana as well. Even when Martha remarried, Mariana continued to live with Aunt Lucretia and Uncle
James.

In the evenings, after the last runny nose had been wiped
and the last glass of water had been carried up the stairs,
Lucretia sank into a chair by the fire to leaf through a book
that Grandfather Mott had written, *On the Education of
Children*. He recommended gentle firmness rather than
whippings. "Young children will seldom need greater punishment than confinement or being deprived of some amusement," he wrote. "Never to give them what they cry for will
be a far more efficacious remedy than to call for *the old
man* or *mad dog* who are to come down the chimney for
naughty children."

Lucretia followed his advice to spare the rod, but she was
careful not to spoil the child either. Her youngsters were
brought up according to Nantucket standards. Each little
girl had her sampler and her daily stint of hemming to finish
while Tom, the only boy, was assigned to the woodbin and
the care of the small yard out back. As the girls grew older,
they helped to make James's shirts and their own dresses. In
the late afternoons, mother and daughters gathered around
the fireplace in the parlor with their sewing much as the
Coffins had done when Lucretia was a girl.

At a time when parents were household dictators and
children were expected to obey orders without questioning,
Lucretia believed that "a child, like all human beings, has
inalienable rights." She enjoyed her children, while they in
turn enjoyed her. Throughout their growing-up years, her
letters were filled with delighted descriptions of their activities.

"Anna is pursuing her Latin study in company with her Yarnall cousins. She is considered forward in her learning for one of her age . . . Maria has begun to go to her cousin Rebecca's school, and is much pleased with learning to write and cipher . . . Elizabeth has six teeth and is very forward on her feet; gets up by chairs and creeps about with rapidity . . . I write with my babe in my arms. I wish you could see what a lovely fat little pet she is. Her father already flatters himself she looks pleased when he takes her . . . I sometimes have three of them in bed with me by daylight in the morning—Thomas, Elizabeth, and Patty . . ."

There were dreary times, of course, when a cranky baby was cutting teeth or coming down with mumps or chicken pox. Once five children had measles in the same week and James wrote to his mother, "My L. seems almost worn out, and I am fearful will be ill herself."

Keeping house for a family of nine before the days of cook stoves and hot-water heaters was a round-the-clock job. But no matter how preoccupied she was with household cares, Lucretia was determined not to become "kitchenified." Her little boy's death had shaken her profoundly, starting her off on a search for life's deeper meanings.

She kept a Bible tucked in the foot of her baby's cradle, and a copy of William Penn's writings spread open on her bed. While she rocked Elizabeth to sleep or held Maria on her lap, she read and memorized passages that interested her. Often she wrote Grandfather Mott to ask his opinion of a Biblical text or to question some Quaker rule of discipline.

Only a short time after little Thomas's death, she had risen in Twelfth Street Meeting and hesitantly offered a prayer. Her first modest prayer was followed by others. As she gained confidence, she developed a conversational speaking style that offered a pleasant contrast to the singsong tones and rambling delivery of many other Friends. It wasn't long before people were talking of "Lucretia's gift in the ministry." She was twenty-eight when the joking prediction that Anna Coffin had made on Nantucket came true. Long-tongued Lucretia who used to mimic the speakers at Yearly Meeting was invited to become an approved minister of the Society of Friends.

Lucretia become a preacher at a time of bitter struggle within the Society. Elias Hicks, the same Elias Hicks whom she had known at Nine Partners, had stirred up a storm by denouncing the prosperous big-city Quakers who were moving closer to the beliefs and customs of their Protestant neighbors. Hicks called for a return to the simple piety of earlier days when Friends depended only on "the inner light" for counseling.

As his uncompromising attacks brought forth angry answers, the Society of Friends began to resemble a society of enemies. Meetings broke up in disorder with men thumping on the floor to express approval or tugging at a neighbor's coat to silence him. At one meeting in Ohio, the clerk's table was splintered to bits and Friends were sent to jail for rioting.

In 1827, Hicks's supporters withdrew from the Philadelphia Yearly Meeting to form a meeting of their own. Similar separations took place elsewhere until the Friends in the United States were divided into two groups, the Hicksites and the Orthodox. As both camps fought for the possession of meeting houses, schools, and even burial grounds, sisters stopped talking to brothers and old friends passed each other on the street without nodding.

From the beginning of the struggle, James and Lucretia had sympathized with Hicks, although she found him "a very narrow man." During the years of unseemly squabbles they had tried to act as peacemakers. When the split finally came, James joined the Hicksites immediately. Lucretia hesitated, reluctant to take sides.

After months of wavering, she at last made up her mind. One First day morning there was a vacant place on the elders bench at the Twelfth Street Meeting. By afternoon the news had traveled across the city and Hicksites were triumphantly announcing, "Ah ha! We have Lucretia!"

She didn't share their feeling of triumph. "It seems almost like death," she said, "to be shut out of the meeting where I loved to go and to see the cold averted looks of Friends whose confidence I once enjoyed."

Even though she began to preach at the new Hicksite meeting house on Cherry Street, she was still troubled by the separation. In her first years as a minister, she had been concerned with obedience to divine law and to the doctrines of her Society. After watching men she respected battling over these doctrines, she no longer accepted them blindly.

Beginning to read more widely, she examined for the first time the works of non-Quaker writers. As she studied, she slowly worked out a philosophy of her own. Wearing the plain clothes of a Friend was less important than the things one did, she decided. Loving God was meaningless unless one also loved men—and this included strangers as well as friends.

"For only he that *doeth* right is righteous," she concluded at last.

But what could a woman *do?*

In those years when her children were small, Lucretia looked at the world around her with fresh eyes. She saw many wrongs that needed righting. Men were imprisoned for debt and hanged for minor crimes. Women were unjustly treated. Wages were low, working hours long, and thousands were jobless. She joined a Society for the Relief and Employment of the Poor, resigning soon afterward, James noted with amusement, because "the conversation at the meetings has not been very interesting or instructive; being too much of what is called gossip."

Then Benjamin Lundy paid a visit to Philadelphia and Lucretia knew the answer to her question.

The greatest wrong of all was slavery. There were two million slaves in the United States. "I felt bound to plead their cause, in season and out, and to aid in every right effort for their emancipation," she said.

10. Making Things Honest

I was indebted to those inestimable friends, James and Lucretia Mott, for a homelike reception, affectionate and delightful. When I was a mere novice in the anti-slavery cause, long before I became identified with it, they were active co-workers with the intrepid pioneer, Benjamin Lundy, for the abolition of slavery.

WILLIAM LLOYD GARRISON

A saddler by trade, Benjamin Lundy had taught himself printing in order to start *The Genius of Universal Emancipation,* one of the country's few anti-slavery journals. Like the pilgrims of old, he walked from town to town with his type in a knapsack on his back, stopping to put out his paper wherever he found an audience.

Lundy had come to Philadelphia to persuade Friends to boycott the products of slave labor. If people would refuse to buy cotton and rice and sugar that slaves had raised, Southern planters might be persuaded to free their slaves. Lundy dreamed of a nationwide chain of Free Produce stores which would sell cloth made from cotton grown on Quaker farms in North Carolina, coffee from Haiti where the slaves had overthrown their masters, molasses from the faraway Sandwich Islands.

Lundy's proposal was not a new one. When Lucretia and James had been at Nine Partners, both Grandfather Mott and Elias Hicks had refrained from using slave products. But the world had changed since then—and so had Lucretia and James.

It was one thing to wear linen shirts in Grandfather Mott's time, when women spun flax thread and wove cloth in their own parlors. It was quite another now that power looms and spinning jennys turned out millions of yards of thread and cloth each year. Even Quaker housewives were tempted by the machine-made cloth which was better and cheaper than anything their mothers had made. Even Quaker merchants were tempted by the profits in the booming new industry.

Lucretia Mott was one of these housewives. James Mott was one of these merchants. In the store that he opened on Front Street in 1823, he bought and sold cotton thread, cotton batting, and bolts of fine muslin and calico. Cotton gave James his first real opportunity to earn a living, and his wife had voiced no criticism.

Now, as she listened to Lundy talk, Lucretia was jolted. He described a slave coffle that he had seen on the highway in Virginia—a line of manacled men and women being driven like cattle to a market in the deep South. "I heard the wail of the captive," Lundy said. "I felt his pang of distress, and the iron entered my soul."

His words were still buzzing in her ears when she attended meeting the next morning. In the silence of the meeting house, she fingered the soft fabric of her dress and pictured the lengths of cloth on the counters of James's store. She too could hear the wail of the captive. Wasn't she helping to forge the chains that bound him?

As a child, Lucretia had snipped a pair of blue bows from her shoes in order to live up to her principles. It was as simple as that—and as difficult. Once again she squirmed on the hard wooden bench until she came to a decision.

"It was like parting with the right hand or the right eye," she later wrote, "but when I left the meeting I yielded to the obligation. For nearly forty years, whatever I did was under the conviction that it was wrong to partake of the products of slave labor."

With her usual energy, she set about "making things honest" in her home. The cakes that she baked were sweetened with "free" sugar and the ice cream she bought came from one of the new Free Produce stores. At her children's birthday parties, she gave out packages of candies containing couplets like:

> Take this, my friend, you need not fear to eat.
> No slave hath toiled to cultivate the sweet.

or

> 'Tis not expedient the slave to free?
> Do what is right—that is expediency!

As a practical shopper who wanted quality for her pennies, Lucretia couldn't blink at the fact that "free" goods were always expensive and often shoddy. When her daughters grew older they grumbled about their "free" muslins and ginghams. "Free calicoes could seldom be called handsome, even by the most enthusiastic; free umbrellas were hideous to look upon, and free candies an abomination," a granddaughter recalled. Lucretia brushed aside their complaints with a ballad of William Cowper's that she had learned as a school girl:

> I own I am shock'd at the purchase of slaves,
> And fear those who buy them and sell them are knaves;
> What I hear of their hardships, their tortures, and groans,
> Is almost enough to draw pity from stones.

> I pity them greatly, but I must be mum,
> For how could we do without sugar and rum?
> Especially sugar, so needful we see;
> What, give up our desserts, our coffee and tea! . . .

Cowper's rhyme answered Anna and Maria, but it couldn't silence Lucretia's inner voice. For James's business continued to prosper. They had a servant now, and were talking of buying a horse and carriage. One summer they had even taken a long-dreamed of vacation, traveling to Ohio to visit Mayhew Folger and returning home by way of Rochester where Sarah Mott and her husband lived.

Lucretia liked her spacious home and the comforts they were able to afford. Above all, she liked the sound of James's springy steps when he walked up the path at night. Remembering the years when he was "down cellar" because of his failure as a breadwinner, she kept silent. But there were moments when she could not meet his eyes, moments when she had to bite her lip to refrain from shouting, "Give it up! Make things honest in thy business, too!"

James was no longer the bashful schoolboy who would do anything to please Lucretia. He was a man, knowing better than she the weight of his responsibilities and the difficulties of a new enterprise. Wrestling with the problem in his own cautious way, he tried to compromise.

In 1826 he became an agent for *The Genius of Universal Emancipation,* and a founding member of the Free Produce Society of Pennsylvania. A year later when he discovered a mill owner who was manufacturing cloth from "free" cotton, Lundy's paper "announced with pleasure that free muslin could be had by the bale at the establishment of James Mott & Co." But he couldn't obtain enough "free" muslin for all of his customers, and he felt obliged to sell slave cotton as well.

His struggle with his conscience lasted until 1830. Then he threw caution to the winds and cleared his counters of cotton finally and forever. After toying with the idea of buying a farm, he became a wool commission merchant.

"From now on," he promised Lucretia, "the cloth that I sell will come from the backs of Pennsylvania's fine free sheep!"

Although the Free Produce stores remained open until the Emancipation Proclamation put them out of business, they were never able to attract the army of buyers that Friend Lundy had dreamed of. For a more powerful weapon against the slave system, Lucretia began to look elsewhere.

Ever since their marriage James had belonged to the Pennsylvania Society for Promoting the Abolition of Slavery, a society which Benjamin Franklin had once headed. Largely a Quaker group, it met to protest the entrance of Missouri into the union as a slave state and petitioned Congress to ban slavery in the new Florida Territory. Most of its efforts were directed toward improving the lot of the free blacks of Philadelphia. The abolitionists operated schools for black boys and girls and lectured their parents on the virtues of Christian life.

Like the society for the Relief and Employment of the Poor, this was worthy work, but it was hardly striking at the roots of slavery. Actually, Philadelphia's abolitionists didn't want to uproot slavery. Not all at once, anyway. They thought that the slaves should be set free gradually, and then sent back to Africa. They could not imagine blacks and whites living side by side on equal terms in the United States.

When she was invited to preach in a black church, Lucretia discovered that blacks thought otherwise. After the service, James Forten, the dean of the city's blacks, talked with her.

"I was born in Philadelphia. I've brought up and educated a family here. Now some ingenious gentlemen have discovered that I'm an African and I am advised to go home. Well, it may be so." He laughed. "Perhaps if I should be set on the shore of that distant land I should recall it and run to the old hut where my forefathers lived a hundred years ago!"

The picture of white-haired James Forten running to an African hut was ludicrous. A veteran of the Revolution, he had invented a method of handling sails which brought him U. S. Navy contracts and a comfortable fortune. It was hard to see why he was not the equal of white men he employed in his sail loft.

Some weeks later when he invited the Motts to attend a lecture at the Franklin Institute, they accepted with alacrity. The speaker of the evening was William Lloyd Garrison, a printer who had been working with Lundy on *The Genius*. Arrested in Baltimore for calling a slave trader "a highway robber and murderer" he had just been released from jail.

Aware of this background, Lucretia had expected a fiery orator of Elias Hicks's stripe. Instead, she was disappointed to see a mild, bespectacled young man who read a prepared speech in what a newspaper the next day described as an "uninviting and defective manner." She overlooked his delivery, however, as she listened to the terrible earnestness of his words.

Accustomed to the Quaker approach which called for loving slaveowners as well as slaves, she was startled by Garrison's forthright attack on "man-stealers." When he denounced the idea of sending freed slaves to Africa and demanded emancipation "not tomorrow or next year but today!" she struggled to suppress a most unladylike "Hear!"

At her invitation, Garrison came to call before he left the city. Over tea, he told the Motts of *The Liberator*, the new weekly that he planned to start in Boston. His aim was to rouse the country from its apathy by telling people what slavery was really like.

"Not in gentle language but in the harshest words I can command. And if I offend, I'm sorry." He leaped to his feet to pace the room. "But the slaveholders have so many friends! I must be the friend of the slaves."

"That's well said." Lucretia warmed to the impetuous young man. Because he was twelve years her junior, she couldn't resist a motherly scolding, however. "Why didn't thou talk like that in the hall the other evening? If thou expects to set forth thy cause by word of mouth, thou must learn to lay aside thy papers and speak from the heart."

James cleared his throat sympathetically, as Garrison blushed. "You are right," he admitted. "I confess I'm timid about talking without a prepared speech in hand."

"Then thou must first emancipate thyself," Lucretia briskly decided. "Think of thy message and the words will come."

Lucretia soon had reason to be proud of her pupil. From its first issue *The Liberator* proclaimed the idea of immediate emancipation. "On this subject I do not want to think or speak or write with moderation," the young editor explained. "Tell a man whose house is on fire to give a moderate alarm; tell him to moderately rescue his wife from the hands of a ravisher—but urge me not to use moderation in a cause like the present. I am in earnest—I will not equivocate, I will not excuse, I will not retreat a single inch—and I WILL BE HEARD!"

The Liberator was heard in every community in the nation. Although its editor never became a great orator, he flayed the conscience of his readers with his pen. He angered many, offended others, and here and there started a man thinking. At last, in December 1833, sixty men from New England, Ohio, and New York journeyed to Philadelphia to hold the first National Anti-Slavery Convention.

11. Philadelphia Winter

*Singularly beautiful in feature and expression,
dressed in the plain but not inelegant garb of a
Friend, she sat among us, quietly listening, occasionally giving in a few well-chosen words her
thoughts on some point under discussion.*

JOHN GREENLEAF WHITTIER

Sister Martha's feelings were hurt. Married to David
Wright, a lawyer from Auburn, New York, she came to
Philadelphia, each winter to see her family. Ordinarily her
arrival set off a series of family celebrations. But 1833 was
no ordinary year. When she reached the city, bubbling
over with impressions of her first breathtaking ride on a
train—at 14 miles an hour—only her bachelor brother,
Thomas, was waiting to greet her. At the Motts, she discovered that she would have to play second fiddle to the
Anti-Slavery Convention.

The back bedroom that was usually hers had been turned
over to two convention delegates, and the welcoming
party—her welcoming party—was being given for William
Lloyd Garrison instead. Every adult in the house, from
her mother to her niece, Anna, was too busy with prepara-
tions to stop and talk to her.

Sharp-tongued Martha poured out her grievances in a
letter to her husband. "Sister L. called on William Lloyd
Garrison, the great man, the lion in the Emancipation
cause, and invited him to tea here. Innumerable jackals
were also invited. There were about fifty, counting our

own family. For a while it was quite interesting till the Garrison and a few of his particular jackals left. The conversation then took a metaphysical turn on the subject of Heaven and its opposite. For the rest of the evening I amused myself with observing the company from the other side of the folding doors.

"The Convention met yesterday to organize themselves—no females present. Several Southern students were there and it was apprehended that they intended to offer violence to the Garrison but he was well fortified and nothing was attempted. I had always supposed he was a colored brother but he isn't.

"Just as I had seated myself to commence this letter, a Friend came to say that he and others were despatched to invite 'the women' to meet with the Convention. Mother, Sister L. and Anna quickly clapped on their bonnets to accept the gallant invitation. Mother urged me to accompany them, thinking my poor letter of no consequence, but I thought I should enjoy myself more with you . . ."

While Martha continued her letter, Lucretia and the two Annas slipped into seats in the rear of the little hall of the Adelphia Building. Busying herself with her knitting, Lucretia listened intently. The men were arguing over the wording of a Declaration of Sentiments. Before she realized what she was doing she was on her feet.

"Friends, I suggest—" She broke off, her cheeks reddening, as a man in the front row gasped.

Outside of Quaker gatherings it was unheard of for a woman to speak in public. The startled delegates stared at the little gray-gowned figure—"a beautiful and graceful woman, with a clear, sweet voice," the convention secretary, John Greenleaf Whittier, noted.

"Go on, ma'am," the chairman encouraged her. "We shall all be glad to hear you."

"I suggest," she continued, "that in the sentence thou has just read 'the Declaration of Independence' should come first and 'the truths of Divine Revelation' last. 'Twill give a better climax if the two phrases are transposed."

One of the younger delegates swiveled around in his seat for a better look at this woman who knew the meaning of the word "transpose." Meanwhile, several men seconded her suggestion.

"And I hope the lady will not hesitate to say all she is moved to during the course of the proceedings," the chairman added with a smile.

Emboldened by this friendly reception, the lady continued to speak on succeeding days. When the delegates were discouraged by the news that two influential Quakers had refused to join their group, it was Lucretia who reminded them that "Right principles are stronger than great names. If our principles are right why wait for those who never have had the courage to maintain the rights of the slave?"

The convention ended with the formation of the American Anti-Slavery Society, "To deliver our land from its deadliest curse and to secure to the colored population all the rights and privileges which belong to them as Americans— come what may to our persons, our interest, or our reputation."

As the delegates crowded around the platform to sign the parchment scroll on which their Declaration of Sentiments had been copied, Lucretia heard a Friend counseling James.

"'Tis all well for these young men to say 'come what may.' But thy business is sure to suffer if it is known that thou signed this document. It would be best to think it over. A little caution, thou knows—"

Lucretia's brow furrowed. Forgetting her usual restraint, she commanded in a loud voice, "James! Put down thy name!"

With a flicker of a smile at his indignant wife, James picked up a pen and signed the Declaration.

Unlike the old Pennsylvania Abolition Society, the American Anti-Slavery Society had a program for action. Its members planned to hire lecturers, circulate pamphlets, and organize societies in every city and town. In ten years time, they calculated, slavery would be abolished.

"With the Declaration of Independence and the Bible and God Himself on our side, how could the contest be any longer protracted?" one man asked.

As their last business before adjourning, the convention formally thanked the women who had attended and "respectfully invited the ladies of the land" to organize their own anti-slavery societies. This was a daring notion. Except for church sewing circles there was no such thing as a woman's organization in the United States.

Lucretia hurried from the hall with shining eyes. The convention ended on a Friday. By the following Monday she had rounded up eighteen women who were interested in forming a Philadelphia Female Anti-Slavery Society. Bonneted and gloved, they trooped into the classroom of a school operated by one of their number. They seated themselves carefully on the low benches, untied their bonnets, threw back their shawls—and waited.

The babble of voices died down until the silence became uncomfortable. Who was to take charge? How should they begin? Even Lucretia was dismayed. Although she was familiar with the Friends' way of "taking the sense" of a meeting, she had no notion of preambles or resolutions or voting.

"There was not a woman capable of taking the chair and organizing that meeting," she ruefully admitted.

They floundered around until Sarah McCrummell, one of the black women present, timidly suggested, "I could fetch my husband. He has an office nearby."

James McCrummell, a surgeon-dentist and a member of the Anti-Slavery Society's Board of Managers, good-naturedly took the chair and advised the ladies on parliamentary procedure. Before the week was out, they met again to hold a formal election of officers and adopt a constitution—which Lucretia Mott was the first to sign.

In 1833, the life expectancy of a woman in the United States was forty years. With the formation of the Philadelphia Female Anti-Slavery Society, forty-year-old Lucretia felt as if she had just begun to live.

12. Remember the Slave!

*We are little aware how the prejudice against color
vanishes as soon as we are disposed to face it. How
little anyone seemed to be thinking whether she
was sitting by black, brown, or white!*

LUCRETIA MOTT

Throughout her stay that winter Martha continued to feel
neglected. While she took Mariana to the glass works and
the Academy of Natural Sciences where a mummy with
real hair was on display, Lucretia ran off to meetings and
lectures. Even at night, Lucretia zealously pursued her
cause. One evening she put everyone to work writing
rhymes, offering a pound cake as a prize for the best cou-
plet on emancipation. On others, she read aloud from the
anti-slavery pamphlets that were heaped high on her center table.

"Sister L. is reading slave laws on one side, Mother
on the other asking sundry questions, so that my ideas
are put to flight and the ink dries in my pen," Martha complained to David.

Only once did she manage to win her sister's undivided
attention. That was when she threatened to go to the thea-
ter. Fanny Kemble, the young English actress who was the
toast of the Atlantic seaboard, was playing in *Romeo and
Juliet*, and Brother Thomas had offered to escort her.

"I mentioned it to Sister L.," Martha wrote her husband,
"but to use rather an undignified expression, I had to haul
in my horns, she made such a fuss."

Usually Martha took an impish delight in Lucretia's "fuss." Disowned by the Friends when she married outside of the Society, she was frankly critical of many Quaker prohibitions. Priding herself on being more worldly than her sister, she read Walter Scott's latest novels and teasingly carried a red handkerchief—until Lucretia presented her with a white one to take its place.

This year, however, the tables were turned. More often than not, Lucretia shocked Martha. For Quaker Lucretia was violating a rigid rule of polite society. It was unconventional enough to speak at black gatherings—"Ethiopian meetings," Martha called them. But Lucretia was paying social calls on blacks and entertaining them in her home!

The barrier between Philadelphia's white and black residents began to crumble during the Anti-Slavery Convention when blacks took part in the discussions, and served as hosts to out-of-town delegates. After a dinner at the Fortens', John Greenleaf Whittier had dedicated one of his first anti-slavery poems "To The Daughters of James Forten":

> . . . And what, my sisters, though upon your brows
> The deeper coloring of your kindred glows
> Shall I less love the workmanship of Him
> Before whose wisdom all our own is dim?
> Shall my heart learn to graduate its thrill?
> Beat for the White, and for the Black be still? . . .

Despite Martha's raised eyebrows, Lucretia found it entirely natural to spend an evening at James Forten's attractive home on Lombard Street or to invite his daughter, Harriet, and her husband, Robert Purvis, to drop by. Purvis, a graduate of Amherst College and a well-to-do gentleman farmer who raised thoroughbred livestock and sheltered runaway slaves at his home outside the city, became a close friend of the Motts.

Although Martha felt uncomfortable at first, she soon learned to accept him. As a matter of fact, her forthright sister gave her little choice. Anyone who disapproved of her black guests, she bluntly announced, "was recommended to stay away!"

In the first years of the Female Anti-Slavery Society, Lucretia served at different times as secretary, vice-president, and president. Whichever office she held, she was always the sparkplug. As secretary, she corresponded with womens' groups forming in other cities and displayed samples of "free" calicoes that a New York store sent her. In the absence of the treasurer she collected the dues—12½¢—and forwarded $10 to the American Anti-Slavery Society. When a winter storm kept the president at home, Lucretia was there to take the chair. And in June when the society recessed because of the danger of the cholera epidemic, she never failed to remind the ladies to "remember the slave" during the hot summer months.

She cautiously felt her way, not yet sure what activities were proper for women. The speakers at their meetings were always men, often one of the Fortens or Robert Purvis. Lucretia noted with interest, however, that among the publications she received, "An Appeal in Favor of That Class of Americans Called Africans," had been written by a woman, Lydia Maria Child of Boston.

To raise money for the anti-slavery pamphlets and for the lecturers who were traveling from town to town, Lucretia organized an Anti-Slavery Sewing Society. Meeting weekly at each other's homes, the Philadelphia ladies made aprons, pincushions, and traveling pockets (gingham bags that took the place of pocketbooks), taking care to embroider each article with an anti-slavery picture and motto. After considerable discussion, for women had never attempted anything like this before, they rented a room and held their first "publick sale of fancy articles."

Before long their modest little sale blossomed into an annual Anti-Slavery Fair. Held before Christmas in a hall in downtown Philadelphia, the Fair became one of the social events of the holiday season. Supplementing their needlework with gifts from sympathetic merchants, and with lecturers and entertainment, the women were able to raise thousands of dollars for the abolitionists' treasury.

Despite the success of the Fairs, many Friends objected to them. Sewing for the needy was admirable, but sales in public halls catered to vanity in a most unseemly way. As the leading Friend in the Female Society, Lucretia bore the brunt of this criticism.

One year when contributions from England arrived too late for the Fair she permitted her daughters to sell them from her parlor. The "fancy articles" included pressed flowers taken from a noted abolitionist's grave and rulers made from a tree under which George Fox, founder of the Society of Friends, had preached. The sale at the Motts brought in $150—but Lucretia had to defend herself against Quaker charges of "frivolity and lightmindedness."

The Female Society also started a school for black children. The school was still in the planning stage when Prudence Crandall arrived in Philadelphia. In 1834, Prudence Crandall was perhaps the most notorious woman and certainly the most notorious school marm in America. Two years earlier she had angered her neighbors by opening an "academy for young ladies and little misses of color" in her home in Connecticut. Stoned, jailed, refused medical attention when she was ill, she kept the school open until her tormentors set it on fire and wrecked the classrooms with iron bars. Only a week after the fire she came to Philadelphia, hoping to open another school there.

"Prudence Crandall!" Lucretia's face lit up when she learned that she was in the city. "She would be just the right teacher for our school."

With the president of the Female Society in tow, she hastened to call on Prudence. Together the three women toured the black section. In a few days they had visited fifty families and had signed up more than enough pupils to warrant opening the school.

The black parents were eager to have Prudence Crandall teach their children—but white Philadelphia wasn't. As the news got around, the brass knocker on the Motts' front door beat an alarmed *rat-tat-tat*. Dr. Joseph Parrish, president of the Pennsylvania Abolition Society, served as spokesman for a stream of visitors.

"Art thou mad?" he scolded. "It's less than a fortnight since Prudence's school was burned. Dost thou want that to happen here? Think of the consequences!"

Even after thinking of the consequences, Lucretia still favored employing Prudence. "But," she ruefully reported, "there was so much opposition to the attempt at this time by a few of our prudent abolitionists that Prudence was induced to leave."

The ladies of the Female Society started their school in rooms on Locust Street, engaging Sarah Douglass, a black teacher, to run it. Prudence Crandall traveled to Illinois before she could find a community that would accept her.

13. Philoprogenitiveness

This is Mrs. Lucretia Mott. Mrs. Mott is a great abolitionist, but she's a fine cook too.

DANIEL NEALL

In spite of her preoccupation with the anti-slavery movement, Lucretia found time for other interests. When George Combe, the phrenologist, lectured in Philadelphia, she invited a group of people to meet him. In the 1830s, phrenology was half-science, half-parlor game. Its supporters believed that the mind was made up of separate "faculties," each located in a different part of the brain. After studying the size and shape of a person's skull and feeling his "bumps," a phrenologist could describe his character.

The Motts' guests nudged each other as Combe went from chair to chair "reading" heads. "Ssh!", James warned when it was Lucretia's turn. He didn't want to miss a word of this analysis.

With practiced fingers, the phrenologist felt his hostess' head. Measuring her skull from ear to ear and from her forehead to the back of her head, he jotted down his findings on a chart that he had brought with him. "Your head is intellectually larger than any woman's I have ever examined," he announced.

While James nodded complacently and Lucretia looked uncomfortable, Combe read off her phrenological chart:

Benevolence:	Large
Combativeness:	Large
Wit:	Large
Tune:	Small
Temperament:	Nervous
Love of approbation:	Very large
Philoprogenitiveness:	Very large

At the beginning of the evening, James had thought that phrenology was a "humbug." Now he was half-convinced that it was true.

Certainly Lucretia was well-endowed with philoprogenitiveness, the phrenologist's word for "love of offspring." Even when her children grew up, she seldom had less than a family of ten to care for. Nor would she have wanted it to be otherwise.

In the 1830s the Motts lived at 136 North Ninth Street, a roomy, old-fashioned house with a big garden and stable in the rear. As their younger children went off to boarding school, their older daughters returned with husbands and babies.

Anna, married to Edward Hopper, a struggling young lawyer, lived with her parents while Maria's husband, Edward M. Davis, bought the house next door. Since the two buildings were connected by a passageway on the second floor, it was hard to tell where one household left off and the other began. Lucretia's grandchildren's earliest memories were of naps taken in her parlor with the click of Great Grandmother Coffin's knitting needles lulling them to sleep.

The four generations got along surprisingly well together. Even in her seventies, Anna Coffin was a vigorous woman with decided opinions of her own. She had long ago started a system of "family sheets," round-robin letters which circulated between Philadelphia, Auburn, and Nantucket, with daughters, aunts, and cousins adding a few lines of news. She liked to read the letters aloud, commenting as she went along.

"Bless me," she would say, "I wouldn't write that for a dollar" or "The old granny! That's not what Martha wants to hear."

Her matter-of-factness, which Lucretia inherited in good measure, occasionally startled the young people. When Maria had her baby vaccinated against smallpox, Great Grandmother Anna looked up from the stocking she was knitting and shook her head.

"It's a pity to be at that expense till thou knows whether she is going to live or not!" she said.

Although Anna Coffin was the grand old lady of the house, Lucretia was its mistress. Two servants and a new cast-iron cooking range in the kitchen made housekeeping easier, but there was still work for everyone. Anna Hopper, the family poet, wrote out her mother's list of "Rules and Regulations for the Household":

> "Our grandmama shall stately sit,
> And, as it suits her, sew or knit;
> Make her own bed, one for our mother,
> And also one for Tom, our brother;
> And when our aunts and cousins call,
> 'Do the agreeable' for all.
>
> Our father, daily at his store
> His work shall do, and when 'tis o'er,
> Return—behind him casting care;
> With slippers on, and lamp in hand,
> Will read the news from every land.
>
> Our mother's charge (when she's at home)
> Shall be bath, store, and dining-room;
> Morning and night she'll wash the delf,
> And place it neatly on the shelf;

To her own room she will attend,
And all the stockings she will mend—
Assist the girls on washing day,
And put the ironed clothes away.

Twice every week shall Edward go,
Through sun and rain, through frost and snow.
And what the market can afford,
Bring home to grace our festive board;
Shall bring in coal the fire to cover,
And go to bed when that is over.

Anna the lamps shall daily fill,
And wash the tumblers if she will;
Shall sweep her room and make beds two,
One for herself, and one for Lu—
Make starch, and starch the ruffles, caps,
Collars and shirts and other traps.

Thomas shall close the house at night,
And see that all is safe and tight;
When snow falls, paths make in the yard—
He cannot call that labor hard;
Wait on the girls whene'er they go
To lectures, unless other beau
Should chance his services to proffer,
And they should chose t'accept the offer.

Our cousin and our sister Lizzie
Shall part of every day be busy;
Their own room they shall put in trim,
And keep our brother's neat for him;
The parlors they must take in care,
And keep all things in order there.
On wash-day set the dinner table,
And help fold clothes where'er they're able.

Thus all their duty may fulfill:
And, if 'tis done with cheerful will,
A sure reward to us will come,
In sharing a most happy home."

"The delf" that Anna referred to were the blue and white dishes from Delft, Holland, that appeared on most Philadelphia dinner tables. Dishwashing, when water had to be heated on the stove, could be an endless chore. Lucretia made it a pleasant one. After breakfast each morning while the servants cleaned up in the kitchen, a little cedar tub filled with steaming water was placed at one end of the dining table. With her daughters' help, Lucretia systematically washed and dried the plates and silverware.

"It was a choice time of the day," her granddaughter, Anna Davis, remembered. "Plans were announced and discussed, letters read and commented on, public events reviewed, and friends were apt to happen in on their way to business to contribute their items of news to the general liveliness."

The same routine was followed at night, even when guests were present. Lucretia presided at the dinner table, frowning at two-and-two side talk and insisting that the good things said should be heard by all. The conversation might range from the "bigotry" of the church to the "real" authorship of Shakespeare's plays or the place of Thomas Jefferson in history. But no matter how high-flown the talk or how distinguished the company, she calmly washed up when the meal was over, flourishing her snowy towel to emphasize a point in debate.

Despite her strong-mindedness, there was a good-natured give-and-take between Lucretia and her grownup children. Although she never changed her own style of dressing, she was tolerant of her daughters' interest in fashions, complaining only if they "wasted good material" in long trains and needless trimmings.

In a letter to Martha she confessed that her household of young people "accept invites to parties where there is dancing and stay far too late in the morning." Dancing troubled her less than the time they spent reading novels. "I long sometimes to see them more interested in reading that would minister to their highest good, but I have ceased to force such reading on them."

Perhaps it was because she "ceased to force" that her children saw eye to eye with her on important issues. In the days of the first Anti-Slavery Sale, Tom was on hand to sweep out the room in the morning while his sisters turned to saleswomen. Anna and Maria continued to be active in the anti-slavery movement, while Edward Davis became a prominent abolitionist speaker—who refrained from wincing when he was introduced as "Lucretia Mott's son-in-law."

In addition to her own large brood, Lucretia was "Mother" to a whole group of young people. No one on Ninth Street could forget the first time Charles Burleigh came to visit. A graduate of Yale, Burleigh had given up a promising law career to defend Prudence Crandall and her school. He was a brilliant speaker and writer, but he had long disheveled hair, a flowing red beard—and a disconcerting habit of putting his feet up on parlor chairs.

Recognizing Charles' abilities, Lucretia set out to reform him. "Thy looks are no small matter," she scolded, "if they render thee, with all thy powerful mind and happy gift of speech, less effective as a spokesman for the slave." Although Charles made the Motts' home his headquarters whenever he was in Philadelphia, Lucretia never convinced him to shave his beard or trim his curly locks. It wasn't for lack of trying, however.

She had better success with another protégé. Twenty-three-year-old James Miller McKim was the delegate who had turned to stare when she spoke at the Anti-Slavery

Convention. A Presbyterian minister, he was beginning to have doubts about the "dry theology" he was preaching. Bombarding him with liberal reading matter, Lucretia helped him to make up his mind to become her kind of practical Christian—an anti-slavery man. By 1836 McKim had resigned his pastorate to work as an agent of the Anti-Slavery Society.

Nor was Lucretia interested only in the development of Miller's mind. After he fell in love with a Quaker girl whose father objected to her marrying outside of the Society, Lucretia played Cupid quite unabashedly.

"What can I do," she asked Miller, "if you young people will come to me, whispering in my ear your heart's best affections? You can't expect one of my temperament to hear them with coldness and indifference."

Offering her parlor as a meeting place, she also spoke to the girl's father on Miller's behalf. When he at last agreed to the match, Lucretia and James congratulated themselves "that we have gained a daughter into the family."

14. A Searching Time

We learn that the assailants objected to a promiscuous association of blacks and whites in this Hall. Every citizen has the right to choose his own company; and if he prefer black to white no one has a right to assail that preference with violence to his person.
Public Ledger and Daily Transcript, May 18, 1838

"Lucretia, thou art going too fast. Thou must call a halt to thy activities."

It was Dr. Parrish speaking, this time in his capacity as the Motts' physician. Running on nervous energy, Lucretia sometimes ran down. In the spring of 1838, when she weighed only ninety-two pounds and was finding it difficult to get out of bed in the morning, James sent for the doctor.

After prescribing a tonic to stimulate his patient's appetite, Dr. Parrish repeated his warning. "Thou art going too far and too fast. I foresee nothing but trouble from the Pennsylvania Hall meetings."

Lucretia crossed the room to pull up the blinds before replying. She disliked dark, heavily curtained rooms. When she was in the parlor she wanted the sunlight to stream in.

"Joseph, thou art not a coward," she replied. "I recall how thou remained in the city tending the sick during the cholera epidemic, while others fled. Why art thou fearful now?"

"I fear mob violence." He waggled a finger close to her face. "Thy foolhardy friends will stir up the city until there's

no telling what will happen. Remember Lovejoy!" On that
ominous note, he strode from the room.

Lucretia stared out of the window. It was hard to imagine violence on quiet Ninth Street. But Dr. Parrish had
some reason to be fearful.

Great strides had been made since the first Anti-Slavery
Convention. Local societies had been formed in every state
of the North. James was a founder of the Pennsylvania Anti-
Slavery Society and in 1837 Lucretia had led a delegation
of seventeen women to New York for a National Convention
of Anti-Slavery Women.

The abolitionists were succeeding in arousing the consciences of their fellow citizens, but they had also aroused a
formidable opposition. In recent years literally hundreds of
abolitionist meetings had been broken up. Garrison had
been dragged through the streets of Boston with a rope
around his waist. Burleigh and Whittier had been pelted
with rocks and rotten eggs. Only six months earlier, Elijah
Lovejoy, an anti-slavery editor in Illinois, had been killed
by an armed mob.

Even Philadelphia had acquired many of the attitudes of
a Southern community. Only forty miles from the slave
states, it was the first port of call for cotton ships. Its hotels
and theaters were filled with vacationing Southerners and
its medical schools with planters' sons. Anxious not to dis-
turb this profitable trade with the South, the city's press
and politicians were increasingly pro-slavery.

Finding it difficult to rent halls for any sort of liberal
meeting, a group of Philadelphians had raised $40,000 to
build an auditorium of their own. Just completed, Pennsylvania Hall was to be dedicated on May 14, "to the rights of
free discussion." After the opening ceremonies, the Conven-

tion of Anti-Slavery Women would meet there—paying what Lucretia considered an exorbitant rental of $25 a day.

The weekend before the dedication, abolitionists from all over the North converged on Philadelphia. Lucretia's daughters watched with dismay as carriage after carriage drove up Ninth Street. The Motts soon had a dozen guests, including Maria Chapman and Mary Parker, leaders of the Boston Female Anti-Slavery Society, and two black women from New England.

No illness could keep Lucretia in bed now. Bustling about, making sure that everyone was comfortable, she even found time to call on Garrison who was staying a few squares away. On First day afternoon she and James took their guests on a tour of the city, driving them past Independence Hall and out to Fairmount Park where the famous waterworks were located.

The following morning the Motts and their visitors walked to Pennsylvania Hall. It was a splendid marble building fronting on Sixth Street, its first floor housing lecture and committee rooms and an office for *The Pennsylvania Freeman*, a new weekly that Whittier was editing. The auditorium on the second floor had seats for 3000 people.

Lucretia wasn't sure that she approved of the elaborate gaslight fixtures, the blue plush chairs and the shiny damask sofa on the platform. It was all a little too glittering for her taste. But certainly no expense had been spared to make Pennsylvania Hall one of the nation's largest and most luxuriant meeting places.

Dr. Parrish, who was Whittier's host, breathed a sigh of relief when the dedication ceremonies were over. David Paul Brown, a noted lawyer, had defended the rights of "fanatics" to be heard. "Were our forefathers fanatics when they declared all men equally free?" he asked. "Who then

are the fanatics? Those who assert the right to discuss subjects of national policy and philanthropy? Or those who
utterly forbid it?"

After Brown's talk, Charles Burleigh read a poem that
Whittier had written for the occasion:

> ". . . This fair Hall to Truth and Freedom given,
> Pledged to the Right before all Earth and Heaven,
> A free arena for the strife of mind,
> To caste, or sect, or color unconfined,
> Shall thrill with echoes such as ne'er of old
> From Roman hall or Grecian temple rolled . . .
>
> Fitting it is that here, where Freedom first
> From her fair feet shook off the Old World's dust . . .
> One Hall should rise redeemed from Slavery's ban,
> One Temple sacred to the rights of Man!"

The program the next day included a temperance lecture,
a debate on "Indian Wrongs," and a literary forum arranged
by the Philadelphia Lyceum. Then came the Convention of
Anti-Slavery Women—and trouble.

Placards calling attention to the convention had been
posted throughout downtown Philadelphia. Citizens with "a
proper respect for the right of property and the preservation of the Constitution" were asked to "demand the immediate dispersion of said convention, forcibly if they must."

Lucretia noticed a knot of men and boys on Sixth Street
as she entered the hall. Upstairs the women were less agi-
tated by these strangers than by their male abolitionist
friends who had taken seats in the auditorium. In 1838,
ladies—proper ladies—did not address audiences that included men.

Lucretia frowned as several of the convention's officers
hesitated to speak. When a delegate, blushing scarlet, apolo-

gized for daring to address "a promiscuous assembly" she could no longer contain herself.

"Nonsense!" she interrupted. "I hope that such false notions of delicacy and propriety will not long obtain in this enlightened country."

As the crowd on Sixth Street grew noisier the women became more bold. Drowned out by catcalls from below, slender Maria Chapman pulled her red shawl tighter around her shoulders and prayed aloud for the strength to speak the truth. After stones came crashing through the windows, gray-gowned Lucretia begged the audience to remain steadfast—and steadfast they remained, even when a group of ruffians burst into the room and ran shouting down the center aisle.

Their presence broke up the meeting that day, but the women were back again the next morning, determined to go on. The crowd outside was larger and more menacing. Philadelphia was in the grip of a depression and the unemployed, fearful of black competition for jobs, had joined the pro-slavery forces.

When the worried officers of the Pennsylvania Hall Association appealed to the mayor for police protection, he brushed aside their request. "It's public opinion that makes mobs," he told them. "Ninety-nine out of a hundred with whom I converse are against you."

Late that day as brickbats shattered the auditorium windows, Lucretia Mott was asked to present a message from the officers of the hall. Marching up to the platform she dutifully read:

"The President of the Pennsylvania Hall Association desires the Convention to recommend to their colored sisters not to attend this evening's meeting as the mob seems to direct their malice particularly toward the colored people."

"Now," Lucretia's chin jutted out. "I would like to express my own opinion. Acceding to this request means giving in to the mob. Our colored friends ought *not* to absent themselves this evening. I hope that no person will be alarmed by a little appearance of danger."

She had scarcely taken her seat again where there was a shout from the back of the room.

"*Fire!*"

Smoke was pouring from the first floor offices as men armed with axes and torches broke into the building. The women managed to escape through a side door. They stood across the street watching the destruction. Lucretia had never seen anything like it.

The mob, more than a thousand strong, had taken over the hall. Gathering books and papers from the offices, and ripping blinds from the windows, they built a bonfire on the speakers' platform. To make the fire burn faster, they twisted the gas jets on the walls and aimed them at the flames.

When the State House bell tolled to call out the fire department, the firemen directed their hoses only at neighboring buildings. "The noble firemen to a man refused to throw one drop of water on Pennsylvania Hall," a Southern newspaperman crowed.

All that night, the hall burned. Fearing for Garrison's safety, Robert Purvis smuggled him out of the city in a closed carriage. Whittier, wearing Dr. Parrish's long white great coat and a wig as a disguise, slipped into the burning building in a vain attempt to rescue his papers. By dawn there was nothing left of the hall—"the beautiful temple consecrated to Liberty"—but a mess of blackened rubble.

Brushing away angry tears, Lucretia and her guests considered their next step. Their convention had been scheduled to hold its final session in the morning at Temperance Hall. What should they do? Without a dissenting voice, they decided to continue.

When the trustees of Temperance Hall barred their meeting, the women marched through the streets two-by-two, while a jeering crowd followed. They concluded their business in a little schoolroom on Cherry Street with a history-making resolution:

"Resolved, That prejudice against color is the very spirit of slavery. It is, therefore, the duty of abolitionists to identify themselves with these oppressed Americans, by sitting with them in places of worship, by appearing with them in our streets, by giving them our countenance in steamboats and stages, by visiting them at their homes and encouraging them to visit us, receiving them as we do our white fellow citizens."

Not everyone at the meeting favored the resolution. "Even Mother found her principles and long-cherished predilections sadly at war with each other," Lucretia told Martha. "She wants us to stand firm in this hour of trial and not yield to the mob, but she would far prefer Mary Needles and others acting out our principles to my doing so."

Anna Coffin had real cause for concern. With a mob still roaming the streets, rumors were strong that the Motts' house would be attacked that night. As soon as the convention ended, the Boston ladies took the evening cars for New York. Worn down by the excitement, Maria Chapman was running a fever when she left.

James marveled at his frail little wife's composure. Panicky friends rushed in to urge them to flee, but she went on serving supper in her usual way.

"It was really somewhat ludicrous to hear persons that were all tremulous with agitation, gravely counseling Lucretia to keep cool and avoid undue excitement while she all the time was as cool as a summer morning," Charles Burleigh reported. "I must tell you how frightened Dr. Parrish was. He seemed to think the very preservation of the city depended on people's taking his advice and he gravely counseled that we dissolve our anti-slavery societies and let things jog on in the old way."

When supper was over, Lucretia took up a command post in the center of her parlor. Anticipating a fire, she sent clothing and some light articles of furniture to a friend's while Anna Coffin took the younger children to Maria's. By 8 o'clock, half a dozen men, most of them peace-loving Quakers, were posted at the Motts' ready for any emergency.

Fifteen-year-old Tom who had been out in the street, dashed inside. "They're coming! They're coming!" he shouted.

Lucretia stiffened, listening to the hideous yells of the mob. A crowd of men was pouring up Race Street. She could hear them distinctly as they turned into Ninth, coming closer and closer.

Scarcely breathing, she reached for James's hand. Miraculously, the din grew fainter. The men seemed to be moving away. She later learned that a quick-witted friend had joined them. Shouting "On to the Motts," he had led them in the wrong direction!

Before the anxious night was over, the mob burned a newly built Colored Orphans Home and attacked the office of the *Public Ledger* because the paper had called the Pennsylvania Hall fire "a scandalous outrage against decency." The watchers at the Motts at last concluded that they were to escape a visit. Lucretia and James went upstairs, while Burleigh and another husky young man made up a bed on the parlor floor.

The next day Lucretia was asked how she had felt as the mob approached her door. She answered soberly, "It was a searching time. I had often thought how I should sustain myself if called to pass such an ordeal. I hope I speak not in the spirit of boasting when I tell you I believe I was strengthened by God. I felt willing to suffer whatever the cause required."

15. The Times That Try Men's Souls

If Victoria can be high Admiral of England, the head of her navies and grand marshal of her forces by land, as well as head of the church, surely Lucretia Mott may bear testimony against human slavery in England in a peaceful quiet convention of Christians.

Herald of Freedom, May 30, 1840

The streets of Philadelphia grew quiet, but Dr. Parrish had not yet recovered from his fright. He was sure that the riots were caused by the women's insistence on "amalgamation." Arriving at Lucretia's one afternoon with an armful of Southern newspapers, he begged her to read their accounts of the Pennsylvania Hall meetings.

"Here one correspondent describes 'blacks and whites sitting together in amalgamated ease.' Another says he saw 'a descendant of Africa side by side with some of the fairest and wealthiest daughters of Philadelphia!'"

"And what wouldst thou have had me do, Joseph?" Lucretia gently asked.

Mistaking her mild tone for agreement, he had an answer ready. "Before the minutes of the Women's Convention go to the printers thou must take out that resolution relating to social intercourse with the colored people."

"Joseph!" Lucretia's eyes blazed. "The convention passed that resolution. It would be highly improper for me to withdraw it."

"Improper or no, it's the path of prudence to do so," the doctor persisted. "I'm willing to take the responsibility."

When he found that he could not convince Lucretia to tamper with the convention's minutes, Dr. Parrish called a group of prominent blacks together. Advising them to refuse invitations to white homes, he asked them to issue a statement saying that they didn't want social intercourse with white people.

"This they have not done," Lucretia said. "But it has caused not a little excitement among us."

With the first sultry summer days, the excitement took its toll. When Lucretia's appetite failed and she grew thinner than she had ever been, her worried husband prescribed a water cure. Water, whether taken internally or in the form of hot and cold baths, was thought to relieve many ills. Unable to spare the time for a trip to Nantucket, James did the next best thing and drove her to Long Island.

Staying with friends at Oyster Bay, Lucretia donned a modest bathing dress—the first she had ever owned—and took a daily dip in the calm waters of the Sound. She even ventured waist-deep into the ocean, holding tightly to James's arm for support. Surf-bathing proved so soothing to her jangled nerves that when James's business called him back to Philadelphia, Charles Burleigh offered to act as her escort. Timid about facing the breakers alone, Lucretia was glad to have Charles's company, although she sometimes winced as they walked across the sand together. People could hardly be blamed for staring at the middle-aged Quaker matron who looked proper even in her bathing dress, and her unkempt, bearded companion.

"Our hostess thought we resembled two crazy creatures," she wrote Miller McKim.

The next months passed quietly. Martha paid her annual

visit, dragging everyone outside to watch an eclipse of the sun through pieces of smoked glass and insisting that Lucretia accompany her to the menagerie to see the giraffe that had just arrived from Africa, the first of its kind in the United States.

Except for a toothache that required the application of five Italian leeches to her gums—"they looked killing" Martha said—Lucretia's health continued to improve. She nursed her children through a series of wintertime ailments and took care of Miller McKim when he too, fell sick. By the time spring rolled around, she was ready for action again.

When the anti-slavery women voted to return to Philadelphia, Lucretia volunteered to find a hall for their convention. After the owners of every suitable building—including the city's seven Quaker meeting houses—turned her down, a friend offered her a barnlike structure on Filbert Street that had formerly been used as a riding school.

Shortly before the convention, the mayor of Philadelphia paid her a call. "I'm determined to prevent the recurrence of last year's outrages," he announced.

Over a cup of tea he cautiously came to the point of his visit. "Do you expect colored women to attend? If so, I beg you to avoid all unnecessary walking with them."

Lucretia put down her tea cup with what could almost be described as a bang. "We certainly don't intend a parade," she loftily informed him, "but we shall walk with them as the occasion offers. I have done so repeatedly within the last month and am none the worse for it."

His Honor gulped his tea as she continued. "Since I expect to put up colored delegates from Boston, I shall doubtless accompany them to the meeting place. Would thou have me forget my duties as a hostess to do otherwise?"

The mayor sidestepped the question, breaking his silence only to say that he would station officers at the riding school while the women met.

"As thou wishes." Lucretia refused to unbend. "But remember, we have not asked for thy aid."

Although the meeting was peaceful, 1839 marked the last convention of the anti-slavery women. As Lucretia reported to the Female Society soon afterward, "The fettered mind of woman is fast releasing itself from the thralldom in which long-existing custom has bound it. By the exercise of her talents in the cause of the oppressed her intellectual as well as moral being is rising into new life."

What she was saying in her sometimes wordy way was that there was no longer a need for a separate women's convention. That year the American Anti-Slavery Society had voted to invite "all persons opposed to slavery" to join its ranks—and "persons" now included women!

A small-scale social revolution had been taking place. Abolitionist women were daring to speak in public, not only to members of their own sex, but to "promiscuous assemblies." In many quarters they were roundly condemned for their unnatural behavior. The leading ministers of Massachusetts had issued a Pastoral Letter warning that public speaking threatened the female character with permanent injury. Witty Maria Chapman had answered with a poem that she titled, "The Times That Try Men's Souls":

> Confusion has seized us, and all things go wrong,
>   The women have leaped from 'their spheres',
> And instead of fixed stars, shoot as comets along,
>   And are setting the world by the ears!
> In courses erratic they're wheeling through space,
>   In brainless confusion and meaningless chase.

They've taken a notion to speak for themselves,
  And are wielding the tongue and pen;
They've mounted the rostrum; the termagant elves,
  And—oh horrid!—are talking to men!
With faces unblanched in our presence they come
  To harangue us, they say, in behalf of the dumb.

Our grandmothers' learning consisted of yore
  In spreading their generous boards;
In twisting the distaff, or mopping the floor,
  And obeying the will of their lords.
Now, misses may reason, and think, and debate,
  Till unquestioned submission is quite out of date.

Even abolitionists were far from unanimous on the woman question. When Garrison and his supporters went a step further and elected Lucretia Mott, Maria Chapman, and Lydia Maria Child to the executive committee of the Anti-Slavery Society, a sizable group of men resigned to form a new abolitionist organization. The membership of this "New Org," as it was commonly called, was limited to men.

Although Lucretia agonized over the precious time wasted in quarrels between the two groups, she soon found herself the central figure in a battle that was waged on both sides of the Atlantic. The battle started when British abolitionists organized a World's Anti-Slavery Convention. Inviting "friends of the slave of every nation and clime," they begged their American cousins to send delegates to London. The American Anti-Slavery Society responded by choosing Lucretia Mott as one of its four delegates. When the Massachusetts and Pennsylvania societies also elected women to represent them, the organizers of the convention hurriedly rephrased their invitation.

But by then it was too late to limit the American delegation to "gentlemen." On May 5, 1840, "James Mott and Lady," with six other women from Pennsylvania and New England, sailed for England on the packet ship *Roscoe*.

16. The World's Convention

*The middle of the front seat of the ladies' portion
of the hall was the usual seat of one of the most re-
markable women in the whole assembly. Opinions
differed as to whether Clarkson, O'Connell, Garrison or Birney were the greatest men, but nobody
doubted that Lucretia Mott was the lioness of the
Convention.*

Dublin Weekly Herald, 1840

*As to the lion part, we felt much more that we were
created as sheep for the slaughter.*

LUCRETIA MOTT

Although steamships had begun to make the transatlantic
crossing, people feared that their boilers would explode in
mid-ocean. Still a Coffin from Nantucket, Lucretia had cho-
sen to travel on a sailing vessel. During her first days on the
water, she was humiliated to discover that she could get as
seasick as any landlubber. While James remained on deck
enjoying the rolling and pitching of the ship, she retired to
the Ladies Cabin. In the little, leather-bound diary that she
kept throughout the trip, her first entry read, *"Great storm,
tremendous sea, sublime view—highly enjoyed by those who
were not too sick."*

After she got her sea legs, she divided her time between
walks on deck and conversations with fellow passengers.
She managed to keep a motherly eye on a shipboard romance or two, argue about slavery with former slaveowners
from the West Indies, and visit the steerage where children
were sick with measles. *"Half our number teetotallers,"* she

noted in her diary, *"the others often drinking, though not to great excess; toasts to the Queen, the Ladies, the Captain, the Americans."*

After three weeks on the high seas, the *Roscoe* docked at Liverpool. The Motts and their companions traveled up to London by stagecoach, taking a few days along the way to see sights. Plodding through cathedrals and palaces with the rest of her party, Lucretia's reactions were quite as down-to-earth as her mother's might have been. At Stratford-on-Avon when her companions stood reverently alongside Shakespeare's grave, she refused to be impressed. *"Forgot to weep over it,"* she wrote. *"James stood on it—quite a profanation."*

In London, they lodged at Mark Moore's, a boardinghouse on Queen Street where most of the American delegates were staying. Lucretia scarcely had time to untie her bonnet before British abolitionists and New Org men called. They begged her not to insist on her seat in the convention. Lady delegates, they courteously explained, would lower the dignity of the gathering and heap ridicule on everyone. When Lucretia pointed out that the women, duly elected by their societies, were entitled to take part, tempers began to wear thin.

"Women," a minister loftily informed her "are constitutionally unfit for public meetings with men."

"It's interesting that thou should put it that way," she answered in her best bittersweet manner. "Hast thou ever heard slaveowners talk? They use that phrase to say that colored men are constitutionally unfit to mingle with whites."

The minister stalked away, while a young man standing nearby bit his lip to hide a smile. Wendell Phillips, a Boston abolitionist with a growing reputation as an orator, had never seen Lucretia Mott before, but he admired the way she had demolished her opponent. "She put the silken snapper on her whiplash and proceeded to give the gentlest and yet most cutting rebuke. 'Twas beautifully done," he said.

On the opening day of the convention, James and Lucretia walked with the other Americans to Freemasons' Hall. On the sidewalk out front and in the crowded vestibule, groups of men were excitedly arguing over "those women" from the United States. "The excitement couldn't have been greater," one spectator said, "if the news had come that the French were about to invade England."

Once they were inside, Lucretia and James were parted. James, a delegate from the Pennsylvania Anti-Slavery Society, took his seat on the convention floor while Lucretia was ushered to a gallery in the rear of the auditorium. As if to make sure that the ladies would not indeed invade the convention, they were separated from the men by a bar and low curtain.

Promptly at eleven, Thomas Clarkson called the meeting to order. The tears that Lucretia failed to shed at Shakespeare's grave sprang to her eyes when the eighty-year-old man, lame and nearly blind, entered the room. For it was Clarkson who, fifty years earlier, had roused the world to the horrors of the African slave trade. It was his essay that she had shivered over at Nine Partners.

United in a standing ovation to Clarkson, the convention was torn by angry debate as soon as he withdrew. What should be done with the "goddess delegates" from America?

At breakfast that morning, Ann Phillips had begged her husband not to shilly-shally. Wendell was the first to take the floor with a motion to seat "all persons" with credentials

from an anti-slavery group. Although one gallant Englishman pointed out that Queen Victoria, Britain's sovereign,
was a woman, others declared that woman delegates would
violate not only British custom but "the ordinance of Al-
mighty God." Late that afternoon when a roll call was taken
an overwhelming majority of the men voted to reject the
women.

The decision of the World's Convention to exclude half
of the world from its deliberations by no means ended the
debate. There was still Lucretia Mott to be reckoned with.
Tiny, demure, yet with a devastating way of getting to the
heart of the question, she held court in the ladies' gallery
and in her boarding house.

Many of the great ladies of England—and some of its
great men—sought her out. Lady Byron, widow of the poet,
and Amelia Opie, a popular novelist, joined her during
the convention sessions. Lucretia liked Lady Byron who
treated her to sandwiches and took her to the London
shops, but she was dubious about the Duchess of Suther-
land, another of her titled admirers. Perhaps the Duchess
was sound on the woman question, but she arrived at a
country home where Lucretia was staying in a coach pulled
by four grays, with six liveried servants as outriders. There
was too much of "Where will the Duchess sit?" and "Will
the Duchess like to walk?" for Quaker Lucretia.

Wherever she went, Lucretia was the center of attention. Daniel O'Connell, leader of the Irish liberation movement and a member of Parliament, called at her lodgings
to deplore the injustice done to the women. With a political
shrewdness that matched his own, she asked him to put
his words in writing. When his letter arrived, she turned it
over to *The Liberator* for publication.

Even aging Thomas Clarkson insisted on paying his respects to the American ladies. For once Lucretia forgave her companions—"the girls," she called them—for their sentimentality. After she made a speech of welcome, they swarmed around Clarkson's chair, begging for locks of hair as mementoes. When someone warned that he would be bald if they continued, he waved them on.

"Never mind," he laughed. "Shear away!"

Another of England's famous men was less disposed to be charming. One afternoon Lucretia and James traveled to Chelsea to meet Thomas Carlyle, the crusty philosopher who had greatly influenced Ralph Waldo Emerson. "*Conversation not very satisfactory,*" Lucretia wrote in her diary. "*Anti-abolition—or rather sympathies absorbed in poor at home—more free before we parted—gave us his autograph—talked of Emerson.*"

Perhaps the only one who enjoyed that afternoon was Jane Carlyle. She told another American that her short-tempered husband had been "much pleased with the Quaker lady whose quiet manner had a soothing effect on him."

The attention that Lucretia attracted was not always favorable. The Quakers of England were allied with Orthodox meetings in the United States. Before the Motts' arrival they had been warned against Lucretia and her dangerous Hicksite doctrines. Whenever she spoke in public, zealous Quakers hastened to inform the company that she was not a member of the Society of Friends. Josiah Forster, clerk of the London Yearly Meeting, was so persistent in his disclaimers that one bystander wrote:

> Josiah, Josiah
> Thou seemest all on fire
> In thy zeal for the orthodox creed;

> How bitter thy lot
> To behold Mrs. Mott
> Giving forth to some hetrodox seed.
>
> When she rises to speak
> Grave, lofty and meek
> Thy Quaker soul's all in a fuss.
> And when she is done
> Thou cut off with a run
> Crying 'that woman's not one of us'.

One afternoon a Friend who had asked the Americans to his home for dinner, apologized to Lucretia. "Thou must excuse me for not inviting thee with the rest," he explained, "but I fear thy influence on my children."

Lucretia was disappointed to be shunned by Elizabeth Fry, the courageous prison reformer. Although Mrs. Fry spent nights in Newgate Prison locked in a cell with thieves and murderers she was afraid to be in the room with Lucretia Mott. When they attended the same gatherings she studiously avoided the lady from Philadelphia. If Lucretia was on the lawn, Mrs. Fry was in the house. If Lucretia was in the house, Mrs. Fry remained outdoors.

On an evening when, in a crowded parlor, she was unable to escape, Mrs. Fry offered a prayer. Deploring the separation among American Friends, she was sorry, she said, that people had been led astray by false doctrines. The prayer was so pointedly aimed at Lucretia that the woman next to her whispered, "Now you must pray for her. Pray that her eyes be opened to her bigotry and lack of charity!"

"Oh no," Lucretia shook her head. "Her prayer certainly took unfair advantage of a stranger, but I wouldn't answer it in the home of her friends."

Even Benjamin Haydon, the noted artist who was commissioned to paint a picture of the convention, with life-size portraits of its leading lights, disapproved of Lucretia. When she came to his studio for a sitting she brought with her Robert Douglass, a black portrait painter from Philadelphia who was studying in London. Douglass and his schoolteacher sister, Sarah, had been brought up as Friends, but had left the Arch Street Meeting after being asked to sit on a special bench reserved for black people.

Outwardly polite, Haydon took time to show the artist through his studio. When they left, he wrote in his diary: *"Lucretia Mott, the leader of the delegate women from America, sat. I found her out to have infidel notions, and resolved at once, narrow-minded or not, not to give her the prominent place I first intended."* His huge painting of the convention, which hangs in the National Portrait Gallery in London, includes 138 portraits, but Lucretia Mott's face is only a blob of paint in the background.

The World's Anti-Slavery Convention did not prove to be a landmark in the fight against slavery. With one group of delegates busy "putting down woman" and another fighting the battle of the Orthodox Friends, the Convention spent itself in trifling squabbles. Its most significant business was concluded at Mark Moore's boardinghouse. For it was there that Lucretia Mott and Elizabeth Cady Stanton met.

Twenty-five-year old Elizabeth was spending her honeymoon in London while her husband, Henry Stanton, attended the convention as a delegate from the New Organization. On the ship coming over, Henry's friend, James Birney, took special pains to warn Elizabeth against the strong-minded women who threatened to destroy the anti-slavery movement.

Introduced to Mr. Mott in the boardinghouse parlor, the

young bride was flustered. Should she even shake hands with this dangerous person?

"New Org" and old, the abolitionists seated themselves around the dinner table. While the food was being served, several men launched an attack on the women delegates. Elizabeth listened open-mouthed as Lucretia skillfully answered them, deflating their arguments with gentle humor and her own earnestness.

Elizabeth was still eating her soup when she made a disturbing discovery. The main battle at the convention was to be on woman's rights—and she was on the wrong side. Before the dessert appeared, she had changed sides publicly. While Birney glowered and Henry nudged her under the table, she came to Mrs. Mott's defense.

"I shall never forget the look of recognition she gave me when she saw, by my remarks, that I comprehended the problem of woman's rights and wrongs," Elizabeth later wrote. "How beautiful she looked to me that day!"

The following morning an exasperated James Birney packed his valise and moved to another boardinghouse. Henry Stanton stayed. On the final day of the convention, he was the only New Org man to protest against the rejection of the women delegates.

To Elizabeth, brought up in a proper Presbyterian household where the fear of God and the word of father reigned, Lucretia Mott continued to be a revelation. She was the first woman Elizabeth had met with confidence enough in herself to form her own opinions and to state them. "It seemed to me like meeting a being from some larger planet to find a woman who dared to question the opinions of Popes, Kings, Parliaments with the same freedom that she would criticize an editorial in *The London Times*," she wrote.

Like a school girl with a crush, Elizabeth pursued her new friend. Strolling across London Bridge or visiting the Zoological Gardens with her, she bombarded the older woman with eager questions. At first she eyed Lucretia's plain dress with misgivings. Pretty, curly haired Elizabeth had never talked to a Quaker before. Anxious to make her own position clear, she confessed that she enjoyed novel-reading and dancing.

Instead of scolding her, Lucretia smiled, thinking of her own daughters. "I regard dancing as a very harmless amusement," she answered. "Remember that the Ministers Alliance that passed a resolution declaring dancing a sin tabled another resolution declaring slavery a sin!"

One afternoon when a group of abolitionists toured the British Museum, Elizabeth and Lucretia sat down on a marble bench near the door. They told their companions that they would follow in a few minutes. Three hours went by. When the others returned from their sightseeing, the two women were still on the same bench, having seen nothing but each other.

Whether their conversation ranged from social theories to the bright feathers of the birds in the zoo, it always returned to the topic that had brought them together in the first place—the unequal position of women. As they walked arm in arm down Great Queen Street one evening they resolved to organize a woman's rights convention when they returned home.

Eight years were to pass before they could put their resolution into effect. But when young Elizabeth Stanton was asked what sight had impressed her most on the grand tour that she and Henry made of Great Britain and France, her answer was "Lucretia Mott."

17. From Queen Victoria's Land

*In the history of the world the doctrine of reform
never had such a scope as at the present hour. We
are to revise the whole of our social structure—the
state, the school, religion, marriage, trade, science,
and explore the foundations in our own nature.*

RALPH WALDO EMERSON

After the convention the Motts took a leisurely tour of the
British Isles. Wherever they went, they were "made some-
bodies," Lucretia said. People like George Combe and Harriet Martineau, the writer, who had visited them in Philadelphia, outdid themselves in efforts to be hospitable, and
even strangers showered them with invitations. Asked to
speak on a number of occasions, Lucretia addressed large
public meetings in Glasgow and Dublin.

Most of their time was spent in sightseeing. Curtsying
old ladies guided them through the dungeons and towers
of ancient castles, lecturing them on Britain's storied past.
They explored a cave in Derbyshire with candles in their
hands and saw the bonny banks of Loch Lomond from the
deck of a lake steamer. They visited the colleges at Oxford
and a monument in Ireland that the Druids had built. In
Manchester, they inspected the cotton mills, in Paisley, the
factory where the world-famous shawls were made.

Two Yankees in Queen Victoria's land, they were never
typical tourists. Bright-eyed Lucretia was intensely interested in everyday British life. She described in her diary

the way bread was wrapped in napkins at the dinner table, the nightcaps for gentlemen that a hotel provided, and the oatmeal stirabout served at breakfast. She also noted the pale faces of the child laborers in the cotton mills and the barefooted women who trudged along country roads with bundles on their backs.

Accustomed to the simplicity of Quaker services, she thought the chanting of the boys' choir in St. Paul's Cathedral was "ridiculous." Oxford's colleges impressed her, but she sniffed at schools were the boys studied arithmetic while the girls were busy with "stitching and other nonsense."

She had always looked on England as her mother country. Throughout the trip she met Rotch and Starbuck cousins and saw three-cornered chairs and brass candlesticks that reminded her of Nantucket. But memories of the American Revolution were too green for her to feel comfortable at a celebration of George III's birthday at Eton School. Nor was she anything but critical of the pomp and extravagance of Windsor Castle, home of Britain's rulers. James, writing his own account of the trip, *Three Months in Great Britain*, which was published after they returned home, found the contrast between the palaces of the nobility and the wretched homes of working men "disgusting to an American republican."

Lucretia had one blindspot that her husband didn't share. She was frankly bored by scenery. Nantucket had given her a sailor's interest in the weather. She would study the sky to foretell rain or shifting winds, nodding with satisfaction when her predictions came true. But the pink and gold of the sky at dusk meant only

> Red sky at night
> Sailor's delight.

"It is beautiful," she admitted if someone called her attention to a sunset. "But I should not have noticed it. I have always taken more interest in *human* nature."

Touring Ireland from the top of a stagecoach, she saw the miserable huts of the peasants rather than the emerald green fields around them. On a trip through the Scottish Highlands, her companions were so distressed by her lack of enthusiasm for the scenery that she cheerfully suggested, "Tell me when to admire it!"

When they visited Sir Walter Scott's home, the girls' rapturous sighs only amused Lucretia. Scott, after all, was a novelist, not a true historian like Thomas Carlyle. While the girls sentimentalized over his grave, picking flowers to press and bring home, she lagged behind to eat wild cherries that she found growing in the courtyard.

Late in August the Motts returned to London for a final round of shopping and visiting. Laden down with souvenirs for their family and gifts for the next Anti-Slavery Fair, they boarded the *Patrick Henry* for the trip back to America.

The weather was calmer than on the passage out. Lucretia enjoyed lazy days on deck watching the captain harpoon a porpoise, or scanning the horizon for the sight of a sail. When this inactive life began to pall, she turned her attention to the steerage passengers.

Most of them were Irish emigrants who had left home because of the potato famine. Lucretia saw an opportunity to arm them with the truth about blacks before they were infected by the prejudices of their compatriots in the United States. However, when she attempted to arrange a meeting with them, their spokesman objected to listening to "a woman priest."

A less determined person might have given up, but not

Lucretia. With a mischievous glint in her eyes, she countered the refusal with a suggestion. "Suppose we talk about the possibility of a meeting. Surely no harm can come from such a conversation."

That seemed fair enough. Welcoming any break in the monotony of the trip, the emigrants crowded around her in the dark hold of the ship. Speaking informally, she outlined the talk that she *would* have given *if* they had been willing to attend a meeting. Not until she concluded her account of life in the strange land to which they were going did her audience realize that they "had got the preachment from the woman priest after all."

When the *Patrick Henry* dropped anchor in New York harbor after a passage of twenty-nine days, Lucretia was in better health than she had been for years. The sea air had put color in her cheeks and a few pounds back on her thin frame. Happy to be at home, she took a fresh look at her own country.

Twenty-seven states strong, it was no longer a nation of farmers and fishermen hugging the Atlantic shores. The Conestoga wagons whose bells still jingled on Market Street were heading for the Oregon Trail across the snow-covered mountains to the Pacific. The familiar small world of Franklin and Jefferson had gone, and a new one was struggling to be born.

This new world promised many more creature comforts. All over the East, whirring machines were turning out everything from pins to penny papers. Traveling by ferry and train from New York, the Motts reached Philadelphia in six hours instead of the day and night that the trip had once taken. In her kitchen on Ninth Street, Lucretia used friction matches to light the stove. Coal burned in the parlor grate. Gas lights illuminated the long dining table at night, and an upstairs bathroom had running water and a tinned tub.

The class differences that shocked her in England did not exist in the United States, but a widening gulf between rich and poor made thoughtful people realize that reforms were necessary. President Jackson and his successor, Martin Van Buren, had reformed the banking system, ended imprisonment for debt, and established a ten-hour day for federal employees.

This was only the beginning. Each month new groups were organizing to work for public schools in the East, public lands in the West. Samuel Gridley Howe founded a school for blind and deaf children. Dorothea Dix was investigating the country's overcrowded jails and insane asylums. Some reformers wanted to abolish factories and return to the rural life of a century earlier. Others formed cooperative communities where everyone shared equally in the work. Still others believed that the country's problems would disappear if men gave up whiskey and rum and ate whole wheat bread and fresh vegetables instead.

At the heart of this ground-swell of reform was a movement toward the freeing of the spirit. Ministers like William Ellery Channing, Theodore Parker, and Ralph Waldo Emerson had broken away from Puritan teachings. In place of the doctrines of hell-fire and damnation, they asserted that man was born good and was capable of infinite improvement. This meant that the evils of the world—poverty, illiteracy, slavery—need no longer be accepted as the will of God. Not only could these conditions be changed, it was the duty of true Christians to change them.

Not surprisingly, their radical notions aroused almost as much opposition as the anti-slavery crusade. When Theodore Parker preached that God spoke not through the

Bible or the church, but through man's own drive for good-
ness, a fellow clergyman begged his congregation to pray
for Parker. "We know that we cannot argue him down," he
said, "but Oh Lord, put a hook in his jaw so that he may
not be able to speak!"

After her return from England, Lucretia Mott took her
place as a leader in this reform movement. Freed from
household cares now that her children were older, she began to travel all over the East to preach against "supersti-
tion and bigotry," and for freedom for the slave.

18. A Concern to Speak

No mob could remain a mob where she went. She brings domesticity and common sense and that propriety which every man loves directly into the hurly-burly, and makes every bull ashamed. Her courage is no merit where triumph is so sure.

RALPH WALDO EMERSON

During the winter of 1841, Lucretia traveled through Pennsylvania, New Jersey, and Delaware, talking on the various reforms of the day. It was a part of the Quaker doctrine for a Friend who "felt a concern to speak" to ask for "a minute" from his meeting. This minute, which resembled a letter of introduction, authorized the Friend to visit other cities and to call such meetings "as Truth may direct."

Armed with a minute from her Cherry Street Meeting, she spoke in neighboring communities, not only to Quaker groups but to all who cared to listen. One of the places she visited was Smyrna, in the slave state of Delaware.

Lucretia was no stranger to Smyrna. She had driven there a year earlier with Daniel Neall, a Philadelphia dentist who had married her cousin, Rebecca Bunker. The trip was part honeymoon for the Nealls and part religious visit. Their honeymoon had come to an abrupt end after Lucretia spoke her mind on slavery in Smyrna's meeting house. While they were returning to their lodgings, a crowd of men had seized Dr. Neall. Leaving Rebecca in tears, Lucretia pursued the men to beg them to take her instead.

"If an offense has been committed," she pointed out, "I am the offender."

The leader's eyes bulged. "But you are a woman," he stammered. "We have nothing to say to you."

Her head snapped back as she tried to make herself as tall as possible. "I ask no courtesy at your hands on account of my sex," she proudly answered.

Despite her intervention, the men dragged Dr. Neall away and smeared him with tar and feathers. After a jolting ride on a fence rail, they permitted him to rejoin his wife.

"The scene was truly awful," Lucretia wrote a Boston friend. "Dr. Neall's new wife was not inured to mobs as some of us are—she shook as with an ague fit. It was really a respectable mob and I rejoiced to have no feeling in my heart toward them other than pity and love."

The following year she and James were in Wilmington when she announced her intention of returning to Smyrna. Their host, Thomas Garrett, gave her an appraising look. Was she aware that men had been lynched for far less than she was proposing?

The leader of the Underground Railroad in Delaware, Garrett had seen courage at close range before. "If thou feels that thou must speak to the people of Smyrna, I will drive thee there," he gravely decided.

When they arrived in Smyrna early on First day morning, they found that the main street was crowded with people. Smyrna Friends had been notified that Lucretia was coming, but most of the men who followed her to the meeting were not wearing Quaker gray.

There was a sharp intake of breaths when she began to speak. Would she dare to mention slavery?

She dared—and a man seated on a front bench rose and

angrily stalked from the room. Lucretia's heart skipped a beat for she recognized him as the leader of the mob that had kidnaped Dr. Neall.

The meeting proceeded without a disturbance, but when the Motts and Garretts walked back to their carriage which had been left in front of the town tavern, they found it tipped to one side. The linch-pin fastening the rear wheel to its axle had been removed, and the wheel was lying in the muddy road.

While Garrett set about repairing the carriage, a group of men collected on the piazza of the tavern. It was a blustery February day and both ladies were cold and hungry. Elbowing his way through the crowd, James asked the tavern keeper to give them dinner and feed their horses. Through the open door he could see a blazing fire, and tables that had been set up for Sunday travelers.

Barring the way, the landlord shook his head. "There's too much excitement," he stammered. "I should be obliged if you would excuse me."

Although they faced a long drive before they would find shelter elsewhere, gentle James's only comment was, "I have no doubt that those who were at the meeting are far more mortified at our being denied dinner than we are."

A year later, the Motts again visited the slave states. After attending Yearly Meeting in Baltimore, they drove on to Virginia. Since Nat Turner's slave rebellion in 1831, the borders of the Old Dominion had been closed to abolitionists. Yet Lucretia Mott spoke in Frederickstown, Winchester, Harpers Ferry, and Alexandria. With a sweetness that concealed her strength, with a directness that disarmed her foes, she held seventeen meetings during an eighteen-day tour of the state.

"Our meetings were all well attended," James reported.

"At most, slaveholders were present and heard the 'peculiar institution' spoken of plainly, and themselves rebuked for the robbery and wrong they were committing. Some elderly Friends were fearful lest we might cause an excitement and wanted the subject of slavery let alone, but the younger Friends and the common people heard gladly and acknowledged the truth of what was said."

From Virginia, the Motts crossed the Potomac to Washington where Lucretia proposed to speak in the Hall of Congress. Enlisting the help of John Quincy Adams, one of the few anti-slavery Congressmen, she applied for permission to use the Hall "for a religious exercise." Similar permission was often granted to ministers, but the Speaker of the House, who had heard of Lucretia, refused her the Hall unless she would promise not to mention slavery.

Unwilling to accept his condition, Lucretia arranged to hold her meeting in a church near the Capitol. A two-line notice in the *Daily National Intelligencer*—"Lucretia Mott from Philadelphia will attend Friends' Meeting in this city on Sunday morning next at 11 o'clock and at the Unitarian Church at 7 in the evening"—filled the church to overflowing. Before an audience of Congressmen and government officials, she talked for two hours on the wrongs of American society, wrongs that included religious intolerance, the position of women—and slavery.

"The sensation that attended the speech was like the rumble of an earthquake," one listener wrote. "No man could have said so much and come away alive."

The following day, tall James and tiny Lucretia walked up the White House steps for an interview with President Tyler. Smoothing her skirt as she sat down, Lucretia announced their mission bluntly.

"We have come to talk about emancipation."

Tyler who was a Virginia gentleman as well as a slave-owner expressed polite interest. "I suppose we will come to it some day, but the freed Negroes could not remain in the United States. They would have to be shipped to some colony."

James shook his head. "The South couldn't do without Negro labor," he pointed out. "I feel that they should be left free to choose their location, as other people are."

"Would you be willing to have them at the North?" the President challenged.

"Certainly." Lucretia's answer was positive. "As many as incline to come, although I believe most would prefer to remain on the plantations and work for wages."

As if he were half-convinced Tyler reminded them that the Virginia Legislature had once seriously debated emancipation—"until the Missouri question and other agitations put the cause back."

"Then I hope it is not too late to resume those debates," Lucretia crisply replied.

Searching for a way to placate his visitors the President praised the Friends' stand on slavery. "I have lately read and liked the Baltimore Yearly Meeting's address on the subject."

"Thou liked it?" Lucretia's eyes darkened. Tyler couldn't know that when they were in Baltimore James had argued vigorously against the adoption of this address. "We think that it's calculated to set the slaveholder's conscience at ease. It makes more apology for him than he could dare make for himself."

When he heard this, the President gave up. There was no way that he could please this determined little woman. "I should like to hand Mr. Calhoun over to you!" he exclaimed.

Although Lucretia realized that the President intended a

compliment when he pitted her against Senator John C. Calhoun, slavery's most skilled defender, she refused to be mollified. At the door when Tyler, still courteous, said, "I wish you success in your benevolent enterprises," she knew that her mission to the White House had failed.

"Our hopes of success must not rest on those in power," she wrote afterward, "but on the common people whose servants they are. These hear truth gladly, when free access is obtained to their unprejudiced hearts."

19. Visitors

*Under no circumstances where principle is at stake,
is she heard to ask, 'what is expedient?' 'what is
policy?' 'what will folks say?' but 'what is right?'
This being ascertained, the question with her is
settled, and her pathway made plain.*

JAMES MILLER MCKIM

By the 1840s the Motts' home was a regular port of call for
distinguished visitors to Philadelphia. John Quincy Adams
dropped by on his way to Washington. So did George Ban-
croft, the historian, and Horace Mann, the educational
reformer who won Adams's seat in Congress after the ex-
President died. Mrs. Mann enjoyed her dinner and exchanged recipes with her hostess, but she was shocked by
the Quaker custom of addressing even new acquaintances
by their first names. It distressed her to hear Lucretia call
her husband "Horace" when, after five years of marriage,
she still referred to him as "Mr. Mann."

When Ralph Waldo Emerson arrived in Philadelphia to
deliver a series of lectures, he immediately called on the
Motts. After dining with them and listening to Lucretia
speak in Cherry Street Meeting he wrote an enthusiastic
report to his wife. "She is the handsomest of women; so lovely
so liberal, so refining."

His enthusiasm waned after a second visit when lovely
Lucretia took him to task for being too much the philosopher
and not enough the man of action. In her motherly way—
after all she was ten years older than he—she scolded him

for living out of the world. Although she admired Emerson's writings, he was not flattered to discover that she thought more of his anti-slavery speeches than the scholarly essays that were winning him world renown. In a second letter Emerson wrote, "I like her very well, yet she is not quite enough an abstractionist for me."

In 1842, Charles Dickens' tour of the United States was the sensation of social and literary circles. *Oliver Twist* and *Nicholas Nickleby* had been running serially in American magazines and everyone of importance from President Tyler to the mayors of Boston and New York planned receptions and balls to honor the young author.

Lucretia's daughters begged her to call on him when he came to Philadelphia. Despite the fact that he was a novelist, Lucretia rather approved of Dickens who wrote about ordinary people instead of dukes and lords. "Nevertheless," she explained in a letter, "I did not expect to seek an interview with him nor to invite him here, as he is not quite one of our sort."

Before she finished her letter there was a knock on the door. Mr. and Mrs. Charles Dickens were sending around their card, along with an introduction from a mutual friend who had entertained the Motts in London.

"So now we shall call," Lucretia continued. "Our daughters are in high glee."

Dickens' busy schedule didn't permit him to dine at the Motts, but they made the most of a visit to his hotel. Aware that he was headed for Washington and Richmond, James told him of their own travels in the South and warned him not to be deceived by the hospitality of the slaveowners.

"Do try to get a peep behind the scenes and see how the slaves really live," Lucretia urged.

When Dickens' *American Notes* was published some

months later his popularity took a sudden nosedive. One newspaper described his book as "the most flimsy—the most childish—the most trashy—the most contemptible." The Motts, however, were pleased to discover that he had taken their advice. Roundly denouncing slavery, he had quoted extensively from an abolitionist book that Lucretia had left with him.

More and more, Lucretia began to associate with what Quakers called "the world's people." In Philadelphia, one of her close friends was William Furness, a Unitarian minister who had been a classmate of Emerson's at Harvard. Her friendship with Furness created quite a stir in Quaker circles, but when she invited one of his parishioners to dinner, even Sister Martha was aghast. For Furness's parishioner was the beautiful Fanny Kemble, the actress whom Martha had been forbidden to see in *Romeo and Juliet.*

In 1834, Miss Kemble had forsaken the stage to marry Pierce Butler, a Philadelphian with extensive slave holdings in Georgia. After a winter on his plantation, she returned to the North a convinced abolitionist and an admirer of Mrs. Mott's. In spite of their widely different backgrounds, the two women became friends, continuing to correspond and visit throughout their lives.

They developed an additional bond after Fanny's divorce, when a Pennsylvania judge gave her husband custody of their children. Bitter because she was not permitted to see them until they were twenty-one, she became interested in the fight for woman's rights. Once when Lucretia was visiting, Fanny picked some flowers for her. Unable to find a string with which to tie them, she snatched a ribbon from her hair.

"Here," she said as she arranged the bouquet. "I will tie these with the only thing a married woman can call her own."

Visiting a novelist and entertaining an actress was bad enough, but Lucretia next proceeded to scandalize her friends by taking up with a troupe of singers. The Hutchinson family, known as the Singing Yankees, gave concerts in the country's leading halls. In spite of their top hats, striped silk vests and long-tailed coats of royal blue, they were, in their own fashion, reformers. Their concert repertoire always included such ditties as:

> "King Alcohol is very sly
> A liar from the first
> He'll make you drink until you're dry
> Then drink because you thirst."

and

> "Ho! the car Emancipation
> Rides majestic thro' our Nation,
> Bearing on its train the story,
> Liberty! a nation's glory.
>   Roll it along, roll it along
>   Through the nation,
>   Freedom's car, Emancipation."

Lucretia had at first objected to their presence at anti-slavery conventions, believing that people should attend meetings on principle and not for entertainment. Although her point of view began to change, she did not become friendly with the Hutchinsons until they arrived in Philadelphia to give a series of concerts at the Musical Fund Hall. In their advertisements for the concerts, the singers announced that they would welcome colored listeners. Ordinarily blacks were not permitted in theaters and concert halls in Philadelphia, or in other Northern cities, for that matter, unless they sat upstairs in a separate gallery.

Lucretia and James conferred after reading the advertisement. If the Hutchinsons could break precedent, so could the Motts. For the first time in their lives, they bought tickets to a concert and invited Robert and Harriet Purvis to be their guests.

Arriving early at the hall, the Motts and Purvises sat down together. There was a scattering of blacks in the auditorium—and a policeman, acting on orders from the mayor, marched down the aisle telling them to leave.

The Purvises stayed, and the Hutchinsons sang, but the press the next day was unanimous in its criticism. "It is really time that someone should tell these people," the *Sun* said, "that they are not apostles entrusted with a mission to reform the world, but only a company of common singers."

As a result of the uproar, the Musical Fund Hall trustees informed the Hutchinsons that they could not use the hall again unless they agreed to have policemen at the door to bar black concert-goers. Although it meant a considerable financial loss, the Singing Yankees canceled their remaining concerts and put another advertisement in the papers explaining their reasons.

Before they left the city, Lucretia Mott, who had been brought up to believe that music was a vain pastime, gave a reception for the Hutchinson family. "You are martyrs to a principle," she said in a farewell speech. "Philadelphia has shamed itself forever!"

20. Strangers of a Certain Description

I consecrated myself to preach deliverance of the
captive, to set at liberty them that are bruised.
LUCRETIA MOTT

Not all of the Motts' visitors were famous. Some came se-
cretly in the dark of night, departing in closed carriages before the first rays of the sun brightened the brick path to the
door. In 1838 James had joined Robert Purvis in organizing
a Vigilant Committee. The purpose of the committee was to
"entertain strangers of a certain description" and speed
them to friends farther North. The committee records were
sketchy, but Purvis estimated that nine thousand runaway slaves had passed through Philadelphia by the time
of the Civil War.

Of all of the fugitives who found shelter on Ninth Street,
the most ingenious was Henry Brown, a Richmond slave who
shipped himself to the city by Adams Express. For days the
Vigilant Committee received mysterious messages about "a
package" coming on the 3 A.M. train from the South. Three
mornings in succession Miller McKim went to the depot at
half-past two to watch the freight being unloaded. By the
time a telegram announced YOUR CASE OF GOODS IS SHIPPED
AND WILL ARRIVE TOMORROW, his presence at the station had
begun to arouse suspicion. Edward Davis who frequently
used Adams Express in his business arranged to have one of
the regular drivers call for the case.

At dawn the next day a sleepy expressman carted a

wooden crate from the depot to the Anti-Slavery office on Fifth Street, where members of the Vigilant Committee were waiting. After locking the office door, McKim rapped on the side of the crate.

"All right?" he asked.

From inside came a muffled reply. "All right, sir!"

Sawing through the hickory hoops that bound the box, McKim lifted the lid. A heavy-set young man slowly rose to his feet. Stretching out his hand, he said, "Good morning, gentlemen."

When he had been given breakfast and a bath, Henry Box Brown, as he was forever after known, was brought to the Motts. Lucretia breathlessly took down his history:

"He was employed twisting tobacco and yielded his master $200 or more a year. He had a wife and three children sold from him. This almost broke his heart and he resolved on obtaining his own freedom. He laid by enough to hire a white man to undertake his removal in the box. He had a sore finger and applied oil of vitriol to make it worse, in order to get leave of absence for a few days, so that he would not be missed. He is a large man, weighing nearly two hundred pounds, and was incased in a box two feet long, twenty-three inches wide, and three feet high. Dr. Noble says, if he had been consulted, he should have said it would be impossible for the man to be shut up and live twenty-four hours, the time it took to reach here."

After Brown slept through the morning and told his story again for the benefit of Anna and Maria, Lucretia decided that he needed fresh air. But how were they to provide this? He must remain hidden until his master had given up the chase.

"Friend Brown is close to my size," James suggested. "One of my suits, perhaps—"

The disguise was a perfect one. In James's dark suit and with a broad-brimmed hat to shade his face, Henry Box Brown spent two afternoons sunning himself in the Motts' back yard. Then he was sent to a safer haven in Boston.

In addition to helping runaways, Vigilant Committee members made it their business to inform slaves who were brought to Philadelphia by their masters that they were legally free after they crossed the Mason-Dixon line. On the advice of the Committee, Jane Johnson, a handsome ladies maid, walked away from her owner, taking her two small sons. Her owner, who was the United States Minister to Nicaragua, fought to get them back. Charging that William Still, the black secretary of the Vigilant Committee, and Passmore Williamson, a Quaker, had abducted Jane against her will, he had the two men arrested.

The abolitionists planned their defense with care. On the morning of Still's trial, Lucretia Mott entered the courtroom, accompanied by a tall, heavily veiled stranger. Taking seats on a front bench, they sat in silence while the District Attorney presented his case. Then Still's lawyer rose. In a ringing voice, he called his first witness.

"*Jane Johnson!*"

The courtroom was in a pandemonium. The judge rapped for order as Lucretia's companion walked to the witness chair. Raising her veil, she calmly swore to tell the whole truth, "so help me God."

"Nobody forced me away, nobody pulled me, and nobody led me," she testified. "I went away of my own free will. I always wished to be free. I had rather die than go back."

Although her straightforward statement acquitted William Still, there was an excellent chance that she would be seized by her master's allies when she left the room. As the trial drew to an end, Lucretia and her tall charge rose. Accompanied by Miller McKim, they walked to a carriage that was waiting outside.

"We didn't drive slow coming home," Lucretia told Martha with considerable understatement.

When they reached the Motts', Miller hurried Jane out of a side door where a second carriage was standing. As the two rushed down the hall, it occurred to Lucretia that Jane might be hungry. Filling her arms with crackers and fruit, she bustled after them. There was just time to toss the food into the carriage before Miller drove off. A third change of carriages took place at the McKims' and from there the ex-slave was driven to Anna Hopper's. Still breathless, she was reunited with her sons the following day at a Friend's farm in the country.

"It was a bold and perilous move," the *New York Tribune* reported "but her title to freedom under the laws of the state will hardly again be brought into question."

After the passage of a federal Fugitive Slave Law in 1850, every black's title to freedom could be questioned. According to the law, a slaveowner had only to appear before a U. S. Commissioner and claim a black person as his property. If his identification was satisfactory, the man would be returned to slavery.

In many Northern cities, people refused to obey this law. A group of eminent Bostonians even battered down a courthouse door and spirited a prisoner away. In Philadelphia, abolitionists like the Motts didn't believe in using force. They employed a kind of psychological warfare instead.

Philadelphia's most celebrated fugitive slave case revolved around Daniel Dangerfield, a farm hand who had been living as a free man for many years. When a Maryland planter claimed him as his slave, Dangerfield was brought before Commissioner John C. Longstreth for a hearing. The law of the United States was on the side of the slaveowner—but Dangerfield had Lucretia Mott.

She knew Longstreth as a birthright Quaker. Before the hearing opened, she approached him. In her softest voice she said, "I earnestly hope that thy conscience will not allow thee to send this poor man into slavery."

The Commissioner flushed. Half-rising from his chair, he stammered, "Thee must remember, I am bound by my oath of office to uphold the law."

A line of poetry flashed across her mind. Without changing her expression, she repeated it:

> "But remember
> The traitor to humanity, is the traitor most accursed."

In the crowded hearing room, Lucretia and a group of women from the Female Society seated themselves near the prisoner. Sewing or knitting, they listened intently to every jot of testimony. First came the planter's witnesses, swearing that the man at the bar was the slave they had once known in Maryland. When it was the defendant's turn, his lawyer, Edward Hopper, called up witness after witness to testify to Dangerfield's long residence in Pennsylvania. There was so much testimony on Dangerfield's behalf that the hearing lasted fourteen hours, adjourning at last at 6 in the morning.

All during the long night, Lucretia never left the dingy, overheated room. Facing the Commissioner was the prisoner, in the red flannel shirt and ragged coat that he had been wearing when arrested. Next to him, so close that they could touch hands, was the diminutive figure in gray, her starched cap and collar as spotless as when she had put them on almost twenty-four hours earlier. While her fingers were busy with yarn and needles, her expressive eyes reflected pain, pity, indignation. Without interrupting the flow of testimony she was acting as the Commissioner's conscience.

Longstreth, growing more and more anxious, was not the only one who was aware of the drama. Arriving during the evening, William Furness stood in the doorway watching Lucretia. "She was like an angel of light," he said. "As I looked at her, I felt that Christ was there."

Feeling somewhat the same way, the planter's attorney demanded that Mrs. Mott's chair be moved away from the prisoner's. A bailiff moved it, but in a short time, it somehow found its way back to Dangerfield's side.

At last all the testimony was in. Her knitting lying neglected on her lap, Lucretia stared up at the Commissioner. With all her strength she willed him to give the right verdict.

Pale and perspiring, Longstreth summed up the evidence. "The writ of accusation described the aforementioned slave as being five feet nine inches tall. It has been demonstrated to this court that the prisoner, Daniel Dangerfield, stands five feet ten inches in his boots and five feet eight inches without them.

"I, therefore, as the United States Commissioner, in view of the power vested in me by the government of the United States, do find that the prisoner, Daniel Dangerfield, is not the aforementioned slave, and is therefore free."

Years later the planter's lawyer became Attorney General of the United States. When a friend asked him how he had dared to change his political affiliations, he answered, "Do you think there is anything I dare not do, after facing Lucretia Mott in that courtroom?"

21. Convalescent Years

*You will have some idea of the fatigue my wife has
endured when I tell you that we were absent 69
days, traveled about 2800 miles, attended 71 meetings in most of which Lucretia took part and in
very many she was the only speaker.*

JAMES MOTT

In the spring of 1844, Lucretia was gravely ill. She had been
recuperating from pneumonia when Anna Coffin died
suddenly. In her weakened condition, the shock of her
mother's death brought on what the doctors called inflam-
mation of the brain. Dr. Parrish's two sons, who had taken
over their father's practice after his death, tried leeches,
mustard plasters, and castor oil, but for weeks they de-
spaired for her life.

So many people called at the Anti-Slavery Office to in-
quire about Lucretia that Miller McKim posted a daily
bulletin on the office door. At last came the day when he
could smile as he tacked up the notice:

LUCRETIA MOTT IS BETTER

"She truly is improved," Martha, who had been summoned
from Auburn, told Miller. "She awakened at 2 A.M. and
asked for all the political news!"

Lucretia's long illness added gloom to an already gloomy
household. Anna Coffin's death had shaken them all. Accustomed to seeing her in her straight-backed chair with her
share of the family sewing in her lap—even at seventy-three

she rarely allowed herself the luxury of a rocker—her children and grandchildren had come to think that she would go on forever. In the weeks before she died, she had been helping Mariana sew quilts for her trousseau.

Mariana seemed particularly hard-hit by her grandmother's death. In spite of her engagement to a nice young Philadelphian, she moped as if she had lost her last friend.

"Whatever is the matter, child?" Martha asked one morning when she found Mariana dissolved in tears. "These should be the happiest days in a young girl's life, yet thou art forever crying."

Between sobs, the story slowly came out. Mariana was not in love with her fiancé. She loved Tom Mott. Because they were first cousins they were sure that their parents would never allow them to marry.

"We decided not to see each other," Mariana explained as the tears streamed down her cheeks. "I thought if I was engaged, I could overcome my attachment to Tom. But now I'm more wretched than ever."

Holding her daughter in her arms, Martha sighed. How difficult it sometimes was to be young. "Thou dunce!" she gently chided. "First thou must break thy engagement. Then we'll talk about thee and Tom."

Mariana dabbed at her eyes. "But what will Aunt Lucretia say?"

What would Lucretia say? "I'll speak to her as soon as she's better," Martha promised. "But thou must be patient. Remember, the doctor said her nerves aren't strong enough for any excitement."

Lucretia was sitting up in bed with an alert expression on her face when Martha brought in her lunch tray. "I'm worried about Mariana" she announced. "Hast thou noticed how moody she has become?"

When she persisted in her questions, Martha sank down into the chair beside the bed and told the story. Lucretia punctuated the account with exclamations:

"Those poor children!"

"That close-mouthed boy of mine!"

"How could he have concealed his feelings so that I didn't guess?"

"Perhaps it's because thou has neglected thy study of the ladies' magazines." Now that she was talking to her sister, Martha felt relieved enough to joke. "Any novel reader would have recognized the signs of a broken heart."

Ignoring the teasing, Lucretia continued to shake her head. She had been the confidante in so many youthful affairs, but her own son and niece had failed to come to her.

"How little they knew me," she mourned, "to suppose that I should oppose them if their hearts are so deeply interested."

She was swinging her legs over the side of the bed, preparing to take charge when Martha stopped her. "Thy job is to get well," she insisted. "James and I will handle our young lovers."

When James came home from the store that afternoon, they talked the problem over. "Doctors somewhat advise against the marriage of first cousins," he thought "but the relationship doesn't seem of sufficient importance to weigh against their happiness."

By the time Lucretia had moved from her bed to the sofa in the sitting room, Mariana was all dimples and smiles. Her engagement was broken, her gifts returned, and Tom was hard at work at his father's store so that he would be able to support a wife.

Lucretia's recovery was slow. Suffering from dyspepsia

which kept her from sleeping at night, she wasn't well enough to leave Philadelphia for three years. This convalescent period saw many changes in her household. Even before Tom and Mariana's marriage, Anna and Edward Hopper moved from Ninth Street to a home of their own, and Elizabeth married Thomas Cavender.

With only Patty left at home, Lucretia took over her mother's place as head of the Coffin clan. Starting a system of family meetings, she brought together all of the descendants of Grandfather Coffin and Grandfather Folger who lived in the vicinity of Philadelphia. In alphabetical order, beginning with her niece, Anna Brown, and ending with Sister Elizabeth Yarnall, the women met at each other's homes on Fifth day afternoons. Each brought along her sewing, as well as letters of general interest.

At tea time, husbands and uncles joined them. Then the grandchildren—the Motts had seven by 1846—who had been looking longingly through the parlor door were allowed to come in. As it grew dark they played such games as anagrams and proverbs, or read aloud verses that members of the family had written.

In a letter to Auburn, Lucretia recounted the work that went into one of these festive occasions. "Our family party was pleasant; fifteen at dinner and twenty at tea. I worked like a beaver that morning so as to be ready to sit down with them early; did my sweeping and dusting, raking the grass plat, etc., made milk biscuit, a plum pudding and a lemon pudding. Mariana and Patty made cake the day before . . ."

She was never so pleased as when somebody praised her cooking. When the editor of *The United States Gazette* wrote an article that poked fun at corn pudding, a Nantucket specialty, he not only ate his words, but a pudding that Lucretia baked for him. Confessing his error, he gallantly commented that "much which seems repulsive has, when presented by Mrs. Mott, been found palatable and nutritious."

A break in the family circle came when brother Thomas Coffin died of cholera. Lucretia nursed him until his death and then had his body brought to her home for the funeral. When friends warned that she was being imprudent, in view of the contagious nature of his disease, she wrote Martha, "How differently people are constituted! I loved to be with Thomas and to do for him all that I could in laying him out. I helped lift him into his coffin."

With her own special blend of sentiment and common sense, she also removed Thomas's false teeth—"rather than bury uselessly $15 worth of old gold"—and saw to it that his black walnut coffin was wadded with "free" cotton.

In the years that she was not well enough to travel, she found many causes to occupy her at home. Whether it was a collection for the survivors of a devastating fire on Nantucket, aid for handloom weavers who were striking for higher wages, or a course of anatomy lectures, time never hung heavy on her hands.

Teaching anatomy to women was new in the 1840s. There was considerable question whether a modest girl could even study botany, learning about the male and female parts of a flower, without losing her delicacy. When the first anatomy lectures were given in Philadelphia, and the speaker used a manikin to illustrate her talk, ladies fainted or fled from the room. Lucretia and her daughters were made of sterner stuff. After sitting through the lectures, they helped organize the Women's Medical College of Pennsylvania, one of the first institutions of its kind in the country.

In addition to these new preoccupations, she was still

busy with anti-slavery work. Although Congress had passed a law outlawing the slave trade many years before, the law was frequently violated. In 1846 the *Pons*, a barque from Philadelphia carrying a cargo of nine hundred slaves, was captured off the coast of Africa by the United States Navy vessel *Yorktown*. The slaves were set free, and the crew of the slave ship was brought back to Philadelphia to stand trial. The presence of the *Pons* in Philadelphia, its decks still stained with the blood of kidnaped Africans, was a dramatic illustration of the evils of slavery.

Calling a meeting on the wharf in full view of the slave ship, the abolitionists interested several thousand people in their appeals. "All the horrid details of the wretched captives have created a sensation among our quiet-loving inhabitants," Lucretia wrote.

By 1847 she was her old self again. In May, James traveled with her to Boston to attend a Council of Reformers at Theodore Parker's home. The Council included such old friends as William Lloyd Garrison, Ralph Waldo Emerson, and Wendell Phillips, as well as several people Lucretia had never met before. She was glad to make the acquaintance of Charles Sumner, a young lawyer who had recently made a series of eloquent speeches against war. When Sumner was elected to the Senate four years later, Theodore Parker begged him to become "the Senator with a conscience"—and so he proved to be.

After a day and an evening at Parker's discussing the principles of reform and the best means of promoting them, the Motts went to Nantucket. Lucretia's eyes grew bright when the New Bedford boat tied up at Straight Wharf. On Main Street, wagons now rumbled over cobblestones instead of sinking up to their rims in sand, but Uncle Rotch's counting house and her old home on Fair Street were unchanged. Staying with Nathaniel Barney, a childhood friend who owned the brick candle factory near the waterfront, she visited Cousin Phoebe and Aunt Sarah and spoke on First day in the island's Unitarian church.

This New England visit was only a preliminary round. In August the Motts set out for the West, stopping first at Norristown for a Pennsylvania Anti-Slavery Society meeting. Lucretia spoke in Norristown, but the lion of the occasion was Frederick Douglass, a former slave who had become a powerful spokesman for the abolitionists.

During the dinner recess, Lucretia walked down the street with Douglass. Busy talking, they failed to notice the attention they were attracting. By the time they reached their host's, a string of men was at their heels, shouting angry curses at the tall, dark stranger who dared to walk with a white lady. After dinner, a rowdy crowd followed them to their meeting, continuing to express their displeasure by tossing stones through the windows.

From Norristown the Motts headed for Ohio. Traveling to the West was far more rigorous than traveling in New England. The railroad line ended at Chambersburg, some fifty miles from Pittsburgh. From there the Motts went by stagecoach, river steamer, and canal boat. For a week in Ohio they attended a series of anti-slavery conventions with Douglass and Garrison. In Salem, fifty-four-year-old Lucretia had the novel experience of addressing an audience of 5000 people in a tent.

"I have never seen Mrs. Mott under more favorable circumstances," Douglass reported to the *Anti-Slavery Standard*. "It was admirable to see her rise up in all her elegance and dignity. A slight pause, and all eyes are fixed, and all ears turned—a deep stillness pervades the audience, and her silvery voice, without effort or vehemence, is distinctly heard, even far beyond the vast multitude. Her truthful words came down upon the audience like great drops of summer rain."

His description was particularly apt because Lucretia's speech was punctuated by the rumblings of thunder. Just as she finished, a storm broke and torrential rains poured through the canvas roof, drenching them all.

After resting for a few days at Aunt Mary Folger's home in Massillon, the Motts went to Yearly Meetings in Ohio and Indiana. In Ohio, where most Friends were abolitionists, they were welcomed. But when they reached Indiana a different situation confronted them. Offended by Lucretia's liberal views and by her association with "the world's people," leading Quakers turned their backs on her.

For the first time in their years of traveling, the Motts were obliged to stay at inns instead of Friends' homes. "They say we are employed and paid by the Anti-Slavery Society and therefore we might as well pay board," Lucretia explained.

During Yearly Meeting in Richmond, a woman whom they had known in Philadelphia invited them to dinner. Worn out by her travels, Lucretia was feeling ill. Before they sat down to the table, she had a severe attack of neuralgia. Watching her wince with pain, James asked their host, a doctor, if he could give her some medicine to relieve her.

Flushing, the doctor refused. "Lucretia," he said. "I am so afflicted by thy rebellious spirit that I do not feel that I can prescribe for thee."

A hush fell over the assembled company as James took his wife's arm. "My dear, we had better go," he said. "It's evident that we are not wanted here. Thou will feel more comfortable in our own lodgings."

Reformers, too, are human. As they walked from the house, the woman who had been able to face hostile mobs without flinching burst into tears.

22. Age of Revolutions

The question is often asked, 'What does woman want more than she enjoys?' I answer, she wants to be acknowledged a moral, responsible being. She is seeking not to be governed by laws, in the making of which she has no voice. She is deprived of almost every right in civil society, and is a cipher in the nation.

LUCRETIA MOTT, 1849

In the summer of 1848, Lucretia Mott went to Auburn to see Martha. While she was visiting Friends in the neighboring town of Waterloo, she invited Elizabeth Cady Stanton to spend a day with her. Thrones were toppling in Europe that summer. Gold had just been discovered in a California stream. But the five women who sat together on a tree-shaded porch were preoccupied with domestic problems.

Elizabeth and Henry had moved from Boston to Seneca Falls a year earlier. His work took him away much of the time and the responsibilities of their home and three sons rested on her shoulders.

"I keep the house and grounds in good order, the wardrobes in proper trim, take the boys to dentists, shoemakers, schools," she said, ticking off her chores. "I sew. All that flummering and puffing we put on our dresses, those ruffles on our pillowcases and nightcaps, those rows of stitching on the shirts we make for our lords—"

"Has thou heard of that sewing machine that is being advertised?" Martha who shared Elizabeth's feelings about housework interrupted. "I intend to have one. And a sweeping and dusting machine too if I can find it."

But Elizabeth was looking for more than labor-saving devices. "I'm starving!" the plump young matron dramatically announced. "For days on end I don't talk to anyone but the children. I'm perishing from mental hunger!"

"Numbers of women feel the same way," Lucretia sympathized.

"Then we must do something about it." Elizabeth's face brightened. "We must have that convention for woman's rights that we talked of in London."

Woman's rights? Suddenly everyone was talking at once, recalling woman's wrongs. The more they talked, the more they liked Elizabeth's idea. Before parting for the night, they wrote out a notice for the *Seneca County Courier*:

> WOMAN'S RIGHTS CONVENTION A Convention to discuss the social, civil and religious condition and rights of women, will be held in the Wesleyan Chapel, at Seneca Falls, N.Y., on Wednesday and Thursday, the 19th and 20th of July, current, commencing at 10 o'clock A.M. The public generally are invited to be present on the second day when Lucretia Mott of Philadelphia, and other ladies and gentlemen, will address the Convention.

With July 19 only five days away, the women met at Mary McClintock's house the next morning to prepare a program. Seated around the mahogany table in the parlor —a table that is now a part of the woman's suffrage exhibit in the Smithsonian Institution in Washington—they struggled with a Declaration of Sentiments. How could the grievances of eleven million women be compressed into a few telling lines?

Lucretia suggested using the Anti-Slavery Society's 1833 Declaration as a model, but after she recited it Elizabeth shook her head. Elizabeth had definite literary tastes. She didn't approve of the prose style of the abolitionists. Searching through the McClintocks' bookcase, she found a copy of the Declaration of Independence. "Jefferson said it better than we can. Listen—" Changing a phrase here and there, she began to read:

"We hold these truths to be self-evident: that all men and *women* are created equal; that they are endowed by their Creator with certain inalienable rights; that among these are life, liberty, and the pursuit of happiness . . .

"The history of mankind is a history of repeated injuries and usurpations on the part of man toward woman, having in direct object the establishment of an absolute tyranny over her. To prove this, let facts be submitted to a candid world . . ."

In place of Jefferson's list of eighteen grievances against King George, the women gravely enumerated eighteen wrongs perpetrated by men. Man had deprived woman of citizenship and property rights. He had denied her educational opportunities and a chance for profitable employment.

As the final item in the catalogue of wrongs, Elizabeth wrote, "He has endeavored, in every way that he could, to destroy her confidence in her own powers, to lessen her self-respect, and to make her willing to lead a dependent and abject life."

By the morning of the convention, Elizabeth's own self-confidence was on the wane. Henry contributed to her feeling of panic by leaving town hurriedly when he found that she planned to demand the right to vote. To Elizabeth's dismay, Lucretia agreed with him.

"Lizzie," she scolded. "Thou will make us ridiculous. We must go slowly at first."

By 10 A.M. several dozen men and women were standing outside the little Wesleyan Chapel in Seneca Falls—and outside they remained. The chapel was locked and the minister had gone off for the day with the key!

For Elizabeth, this was the last straw. Perhaps women really weren't as capable as men. But when her nephew managed to climb through a window and unbolt the door, the day grew brighter. James Mott, tall and dignified, presided over the meeting while Lucretia explained its purposes. Then Martha Wright read a humorous sketch that she had written and Elizabeth Stanton made her maiden speech.

On the convention's second day, she spoke again. With crimson cheeks, she proposed that women "secure to themselves their sacred right to the elective franchise." Although many in the audience opposed her, she received unexpected support from Frederick Douglass. Douglass was keenly aware of the importance of the ballot, which most Northern states denied to blacks. After he spoke in favor of political equality for all, Elizabeth's resolution passed by a narrow margin.

At the end of the convention, a third of the audience—sixty-eight women and thirty-two men—stepped forward to sign the Declaration of Sentiments, and Lucretia Mott's name led the list.

Only weeks after the Seneca Falls meeting, a second convention was held in Rochester. The meeting got off to a bad start when the voice of the secretary failed to carry beyond the front row. As the audience shouted "Louder!" the president begged for patience.

"Friends," she said, "we present ourselves here before you as an oppressed class, with trembling frames and faltering tongues. We do not expect to be able to speak so as to be heard by all. We trust that you will bear with our weakness now in the infancy of the movement."

"Twaddle!" Lucretia murmured. If women were to enter public life, they could ask for no concessions. "It is the duty of the speaker to make herself heard," she advised the convention. "The secretary should speak louder."

The problem was momentarily solved by substituting a schoolteacher for the faint-voiced secretary, but it continued to plague women's gatherings. In a letter to Martha, Lucretia described a meeting at which Catherine Beecher spoke. "She addressed them well—only in too low a tone— it takes a Quaker woman to raise her voice!"

Throughout the Rochester convention, Lucretia took the floor. She deflated a minister by quoting the Bible at him. She silenced a second speaker who said that women were inferior by sweetly asking, "Does one man have fewer rights than another because his intellect is inferior? If not, why should a woman?"

When William Nell, a black historian, took the opposite tack and gallantly asserted women's superiority, she was equally stern. Rejecting his flattery, she said, "Woman is now sufficiently advanced to prefer justice to compliments."

The two conventions inspired a rash of newspaper headlines: INSURRECTION AMONG WOMEN . . . REIGN OF THE PETTICOATS . . . HEN CONVENTION. "This is the age of revolutions," James Gordon Bennett wrote in a sarcastic editorial in the *New York Herald.* "By the intelligence we have lately received the work of revolution is no longer confined to the Old World nor to the masculine gender . . . The Convention of Seneca Falls has appealed to the country. Miss Lucretia Mott has propounded the principles of the party. If it be the general impression that this lady is a more eligible candidate for the Presidential chair than McClean or Cass, Van Buren or old 'Rough and Ready,' then let the Salic laws be abolished forthwith from this great Republic. We are much mistaken if Lucretia would not make a better President than some of those who have lately tenanted the White House."

"Of course you would," Elizabeth wrote when she mailed the clipping to Philadelphia. "I fully agree with Mr. Bennett's closing lines, even if you may not."

The pro-slavery *Herald* continued to hammer away, attacking Lucretia as an abolitionist as well as an advocate of woman's rights. In another editorial Bennett likened her to her legendary Roman namesake whose rape and suicide had inspired the Tarquin Wars. "The Roman Lucretia changed the form of government in her day. Our Yankee Lucretia is no doubt ambitious to follow the example of her great prototype. Lucretia the first raised a republic. Lucretia the second is bent on ruining one. In these days of violent political eruptions, we would seriously recommend the friends of the constitution to keep their eyes on Lucy, and see that she has no suicidal dagger concealed under her clothes . . . There is no knowing but she might get a Brutus, or a brute of some sort or other, to avenge her wrongs and involve us in all the horrors of anarchy and insurrection."

The ridicule heaped on the Seneca Falls and Rochester meetings caused many of the original signers of the Declaration to withdraw their names, but the nationwide publicity aroused women everywhere. Before long Woman's Equal Rights Unions and Equal Suffrage Societies were springing up all over the North and West. In 1850 the first National Woman's Rights Convention was held. Despite a *New York Herald* headline, AWFUL COMBINATION OF

SOCIALISM, ABOLITIONISM AND INFIDELITY, it continued to meet annually until the Civil War.

Serving as president or chairwoman of the convention's central committee, Lucretia was the elder statesman of the new movement. Often she took on the task of answering its critics. The *New York Herald's* blasts were shrugged off, but when Richard Henry Dana, a Boston literary light, came to Philadelphia to deliver an "Address on Woman," she was an interested member of his audience. Dana drew on Shakespeare, Milton, and the Bible to prove that women were physically, mentally, and morally weaker than men.

At the end of the lecture, Lucretia went up to talk to him. "Friend Dana," she said, "I consider that thou art wrong in thy representation of women and—"

Instead of hearing her out, Dana fumbled for his hat and hurried from the hall. Piqued by his rudeness, Lucretia made up her mind to answer him publicly. A few days later, in the hall of the Assembly Buildings, she delivered a "Discourse on Woman." Equally scholarly in her approach, she traced women in history, from Old Testament figures to Dorothea Dix and Maria Mitchell, an astronomer who had lately been honored for discovering a comet.

Accustomed to talking in the Quaker way, as the spirit moved her, Lucretia never wrote out her speeches ahead of time. On this occasion, however, a phonographer was in the audience. Using a system of shorthand that had just been devised, he took down her exact words. Her "Discourse," printed as a pamphlet, circulated at women's meetings in the United States and Great Britain for the next twenty years.

Lucretia's relationship with Elizabeth Stanton continued to be one of mutual admiration. Whenever she visited Martha, they drove to Seneca Falls for a council of war.

Despite Elizabeth's complaints that Lucretia toned down her fieriest pronunciamentos, her Quaker friend sometimes surprised her.

After years of lobbying, the women had persuaded New York State's legislature to improve the laws governing women's property rights and the guardianship of their children. Elizabeth next planned to tackle the touchy subject of divorce. Even such old-time reformers as Garrison and Phillips opposed divorce, while Lucy Stone, one of the younger women in the movement, said "It is a great, grave topic that one shudders to grapple." Nevertheless, when a lawmaker introduced the first bill permitting women to divorce their husbands—only if the husbands were habitual drunkards—Elizabeth decided to speak in its favor.

She asked Lucretia to accompany her and Ernestine Rose, another woman's rights leader, to the hearings in Albany. Lucretia agreed, only after cautioning Elizabeth "not to take too radical ground." She had not planned to speak, but as she listened to the testimony she grew more and more indignant. Soon she was delivering a vigorous attack on the law that "bound pure innocent women to dissipated unprincipled men."

As they left the Capitol, her companions shook with laughter. "Lucretia," Elizabeth informed her, "your speech was altogether the most radical of the three."

In addition to fighting for changes in laws, Elizabeth was eager to rid women of the false notions of delicacy which hampered them in their daily lives. In the mid-nineteenth century, a lady stayed at home for a month after having a baby. Elizabeth Stanton didn't. The day after her fifth child was born she went for a three-mile drive.

"Am I not almost a savage?" she wrote Lucretia. "What

refined, delicate, genteel, civilized woman would get well in so indecently short a time?"

"What a woman!" Lucretia cheered. "We who live after the older school methods cannot tell what hardy reformers can bear. I rode out in less than a week after the birth of my children and was classed among the Indians for so rash an act."

Elizabeth also had novel notions about bringing up her children. Recalling her own childhood, she encouraged her youngsters to think for themselves. The results were sometimes dismaying. During one of Lucretia's visits she complained that her boys had learned to swear.

"No punishment that I can devise seems to stop them," she said. Lucretia had a wicked twinkle in her eye as she proposed a strategy. The Stanton boys were trained to wait on the table when guests were present. Paid for their work, they took pride in doing it well. But when Mrs. Mott sweetly asked, "May I have some more of that damned chicken?" platters dropped and spoons slipped from shaky hands.

For three dinners, the ladies peppered the conversation with "damns" and "hells," while the boys' eyes bulged. At the fourth when Senator William Seward and their Congressman cousin, Gerrit Smith, were present to hear the profanity, they had had enough.

"Mother," they scolded as soon as they could get Elizabeth alone. "What will the Senator and Cousin Gerrit think of you, swearing like that!"

"You boys do it," she pointed out, "so we thought we would too. Don't you like it?"

"Oh no," they chorused.

"Very well, then," she said. "If you stop swearing, Mrs. Mott and I will promise to, also."

Another subject that interested Elizabeth was dress reform. Women wore tight stays, tight garters, tight waistbands, topped by layers of billowing petticoats, hoop skirts, and enormous leg o'mutton sleeves. No matter how graceful these outfits looked in the pages of *Godey's Lady's Book*, they made any sort of physical activity impossible.

When Elizabeth's cousin appeared one day in a new outfit—a knee-length skirt worn over Turkish-style trousers which came to the tops of her boots—she whooped with joy. The Turkish pantaloons were nicknamed "bloomers" when Amelia Bloomer, editor of a temperance paper, publicized them. After the first photographs of them appeared in Mrs. Bloomer's paper, hundreds of women—farmers' wives and mill hands as well as lady reformers—tried them out. Charlotte Forten, granddaughter of James, spoke for countless generations of school girls when she exulted in her diary:

"Adopted bloomer costume and ascended the highest cherry tree which being the first feat of the kind ever performed by me, I deem worthy of note. Obtained some fine fruit and felt for the time 'monarch of all I surveyed.'"

Wearing bloomers took considerable courage. In addition to attacks from the press and pulpit, their wearers were sure to be followed by small boys who chanted:

> "Gibbery, gibbery gab
> The women had a confab
> And demanded the rights
> To wear the tights
> Gibbery, gibbery gab."

Even progressive women disapproved of the dress. Arriving in Philadelphia for a meeting, Lucy Stone hesitantly knocked at the Motts' door. What was Lucretia going to say about her bloomer outfit? Lucretia wasn't home, but Anna and Maria answered Lucy in no uncertain terms.

"They took up a regular labor with me to make me abandon the dress. They said they would not go in the street with me, and when Grace Greenwood called, I think it would have been a real relief to them if I had not been there."

She had "a most uncomfortable feeling"—until Lucretia came home and defended her. Although Lucretia never considered wearing bloomers herself she had always disapproved of what she called "the ridiculous Paris fashionables." Besides, as she pointed out to her more conventional daughters, "There are so few to advocate woman's cause, it is needful for some to be ultra."

On the morning of their meeting, Lucretia and Lucy went to the hall together. Almost the same size, they made quite a sight as they walked up to the platform—Mrs. Mott in her slate-colored silk and prim cap, arm-in-arm with bloomer-clad Lucy.

23. On the Move

As to 'taking a long breath', it is what I have not done since the Convention of 1833—rather since the separation in 1827—indeed to speak the truth, since I was born.

LUCRETIA MOTT, 1856

When she was sixty, Lucretia confided to Nathaniel Barney who was the same age, "Now that three-score years are mine the prospect of resting, even though not on laurels, is delightful. I was admonished years ago that at sixty it would be time for me to give place to the younger. Now that so many able women are in the field, the 'gift' may be yielded to them without regret."

Undoubtedly she meant what she said. During the next twenty years she retired many times—but never for long.

Soon after her sixtieth birthday she and James went to New York with pockets filled with delegates' credentials. The Anti-Slavery Society, the Whole World's Temperance Convention (organized when a World's Temperance Convention rejected women delegates), and the National Woman's Rights Convention were holding meetings during the same week. There was also a World's Fair in town—the first World's Fair in the United States—but the Motts had no time to visit it.

"The Woman's Wrong Convention," as the *Herald* dubbed it, met in the Tabernacle, a hall on lower Broadway. As soon as she walked into the building Lucretia smelled trouble. Every one of the hall's two thousand seats was taken, but the men leaning over the balcony rail didn't resemble any reformers she knew.

Elected president of the convention, she quickly found her suspicions confirmed. Each speaker was interrupted by boos and hisses from the balcony. In the evening, when Horace Greeley, editor of the liberal *New York Tribune,* attempted to reason with the hecklers, there was a brief exchange of blows. The second day's session was even noisier, rising to a climax when Sojourner Truth, a former slave, mounted to the rostrum.

Tall Sojourner stood next to Lucretia, waiting for the hisses to subside. "I see that some of you have got the spirit of a goose and some the spirit of a snake," she said. "I know that it feels a kind of hissing and tickling like to see a colored woman get up and tell you about woman's rights. We have been thrown down so low that nobody thought we'd ever get up. But we have been long enough trodden now."

Her words were the last the audience was able to hear. When catcalls drowned out the next speaker, a man on the platform advised Lucretia to adjourn.

She stubbornly shook her head. "When the hour fixed for adjournment comes, I will adjourn the meeting. Not before."

Although she persisted in trying to keep order, even a Quaker woman couldn't make herself heard above the "shouting, yelling, screaming, bellowing, laughing, stamping," that the convention secretary next recorded. After hours of this tumult, the executive committee decided to ask the police for help.

As it was against Lucretia's principles to call on the police, she turned the chair over to Ernestine Rose. Despite the presence of patrolmen in the hall, Mrs. Rose had little better luck. That evening, after thanking Lucretia Mott "for the grace, firmness, ability, and courtesy with which she has discharged her arduous duties" the convention adjourned.

While the *Tribune* condemned this suppression of free speech, the *Herald* applauded the meeting's abrupt end as "a great day for New York." Hitting rather below the belt, Bennett's paper said, "These women are entirely devoid of personal attraction. They are generally thin maiden ladies or women who have been disappointed in their endeavors to appropriate the breeches and the rights of their unlucky lords."

Lucretia had met Isaiah Rynders, the Tammany politician who was the moving spirit of the mob, several years earlier when he and his cohorts had broken up an anti-slavery convention. Despite his actions, she felt that he was not all bad—a feeling that he surprisingly reciprocated. When she saw him in a restaurant a day or two later she sat down at his table and talked to him. As she left he turned to Miller McKim, her companion, to ask, "Is she your mother?"

"No," Miller answered.

The puzzled politician scratched his head for a moment. "Well, she's a good sensible woman," he said.

After the New York conventions, the Motts and Martha set out on another trip to the West. Lucretia spoke at woman's rights meetings in Cleveland and in several Ohio cities. On their way home, the trio took an Ohio River boat to Maysville, Kentucky, where relatives of Martha's first husband lived. In spite of their host's anxious wish that Lucretia avoid mentioning abolition, she held two meetings in the local courthouse.

"What will be the result of a visit from this female fanatic is not yet known," the *Maysville Express* said. "We should not be surprised, however, if it were the prelude to a heavy loss on the part of the slaveholders of the county, as a score or two of blacks were present to behold and hear this brazen infidel in her treason against God and her country."

This Western trip was made in grand style, on a train that whirled them across the plains at forty miles an hour. On other occasions Lucretia still turned to more primitive means of transportation. With considerable pride she recounted her adventures after a woman's rights meeting in New York State.

"Our landlord furnished me with a horse and buggy and a good driver and at 10 o'clock I parted with our friends and rode twelve miles over a plank road—the wildest scenery imaginable—numerous waterfalls and rapids and precipitous cliffs. Mine host had lent me a large wadded coat, his late wife's I concluded, without which and all my shawls I should have suffered. The full moon so beautiful— I always like to ride at night.

"We arrived at Conestota after 1:30. The cars would not be along until 4 o'clock. Before four I was dozing a little in my chair when there went the train, not having whistled or halted. Another nap brought breakfast and at eight the other train puffed along and I with it. Reached Albany at 3:30—passage down river in *Oregon*. Retired at eight, slept soundly until three, arrived at New York at 5 A.M. Took the 6 o'clock cars. Reached home at twelve.

"A cup of popcorn and another of peanuts were the extent of outlay for the inner man after that breakfast at Conestota when I spread a slice of bread to eat on the road —it with ice water and the groundnuts constituted my supper.

"In New York after depositing trunk and obtaining ticket,

time allowed a pursuit for breakfast. Meeting a lot of miserable Irish emigrants who had been several days waiting for friends from Michigan I divided my few remaining pence with them and took an alehouse cup of coffee standing—spreading a slice to eat in secret while crossing the ferry. Felt satisfied except that the saucer in which I endeavored to cool the coffee was a trifle spirity."

The picture of their reformer mother, who preached abstinence from intoxicating beverages, drinking "spirity" coffee made her children roar with laughter—as she had known it would. "It formed a merry topic of conversation for a while," she told Martha. "Thomas Cavender said now he should feel at liberty to go into any oyster cellar he pleased."

Even in Philadelphia, travel could sometimes be rugged. On one cold January day, when snow blanketed the streets and the Delaware was frozen from bank to bank, Lucretia decided to visit her niece Anna Brown. Anna and her husband, Walter, lived on the outskirts of the city, a considerable distance from the new horse-car line.

Although her family begged her to wait for warmer weather, Lucretia refused. Anna's children were sick. Besides, she answered with her mother's favorite saying, "Put-offs never accomplish!"

Setting out in a hired carriage, she was close to the Browns when the carriage bogged down in the deep snow. Then sixty-three-year-old Lucretia walked the rest of the way.

"I trudged along feeling so nice and independent," she said. "I could hold my skirts up as high as I pleased and the exercise was just what I needed after four or five days quiet sitting—until cramp affected my feet and legs. The winding road however romantic in summer was then robbed of all its poetry. Even the driven snow, so white, only added to the stern reality of a winter's travel."

In spite of the pain, she was delighted with the dramatic entrance she made. "They were at the tea table. Walter was just telling Anna how very poorly Aunt Lucretia was when in she walked—such exclamations!"

When she was not off on a "wild excursion," Lucretia showed few signs of slowing down. Home in the 1850s was a big red brick house at 338 Arch Street. Seen from the outside, 338 was a typical Philadelphia town house. Inside, every room bore the unmistakable stamp of its mistress.

In the broad entrance hall were two comfortable arm chairs—"beggars' chairs," the grandchildren called them—where someone was always waiting for Mrs. Mott. The twin parlors, connected by folding doors, were furnished simply, with mahogany and black haircloth chairs and sofas. Bright carpets on the floors gave the rooms their air of comfort and everyday use. Lucretia cordially disliked what she called "dingy carpets." She still made the carpeting herself, out of rags and scraps of cloth, as Anna Coffin had done on Nantucket.

Upstairs there was a spacious dining room and bedrooms galore. Several years earlier Edward Davis and Tom Mott had bought a farm together outside of Philadelphia. Their two families spent summers on Oak Farm and lived in the winter with James and Lucretia. When Patty married George Lord, the Lords also became regular residents of the Arch Street house.

In addition to Patty's baby in the nursery, Lucretia took charge of Bel Mott and her younger sister, Emily, when Tom and Mariana toured Europe in 1855. Like any doting grandmother, she sent Martha a copy of Bel's first misspelled letter and told her of a newpaper that Maria's son,

Henry was planning—"to be called the *Sun* or the *Comet,* the motto to be 'from little vines some pumpkins grow.' The subscribers—3 cents a year—are mostly in the Davis and Mott family."

Along with the little ones, a new generation of teenagers was growing up. Ellen and Willie Wright, Martha's daughter and son, went to the same boarding school that the Purvis and McKim children attended. During the holidays, the young people converged on 338. Once again, Lucretia found herself involved with clothes and beaux—and with parties where the boys and girls danced while a violinist played.

In letters to Martha she described a flounced dress that Lu Hopper made out of some old black drapes, complained of the hoop skirts that the girls were wearing and mentioned Ellen's "forwardness" in writing to boys. "Don't think it anything of the least consequence," she counseled her sister, "but I find her young cousins begging her to desist."

The girls taught Grandmother Lucretia how to work a sewing machine and persuaded her to try the India rubber sandals that were just appearing in the stores. "But I don't like to wear them," she said. "They make my feet cold. If I wet my shoes and feet a little, nature soon dries them." Although they never convinced her to attend "the foolish opera" with them, she swallowed her prejudices sufficiently to watch Ellen and Lucy McKim act in a school play.

Perhaps the most startling innovation at 338 was a piano that stood in a corner of the parlor. While Lu Hopper or Anna Davis played simple melodies, Lucretia hummed along with them. She even learned the words, if not the tunes, of such current song hits as "Old Folks at Home" and "Jeannie with the Light Brown Hair."

Three-thirty-eight was headquarters for the reformers whenever a convention was held in Philadelphia. Everyone from Theodore Parker and Henry Ward Beecher to Garrison and Phillips stayed with the Motts. Sometimes there were so many unexpected guests that James went to a neighbor's to sleep while Lucretia squeezed into bed with two of her granddaughters. During Fair Week before Christmas, the Motts often had forty at dinner, with the children at a side table.

"Is your house India rubber?" William Furness marveled when he entered the crowded parlor one evening.

Even the new India rubber couldn't stretch indefinitely. By 1856 Lucretia was weary. She was tried of presiding at meetings, tired of entertaining, tired of strangers who dropped in at any hour of the day or night. She was again losing weight and suffering from pains in her stomach and sides. That summer James took her away for a real vacation, traveling first to Nantucket and then to the Flume House, a fashionable hotel in the White Mountains. Sister Elizabeth joined them there and they begged Martha to come too.

"Can't you turn something into gold? Sell one cow and come," Lucretia wrote.

At Flume House, she managed to relax and enjoy the mountain scenery. One day everyone drove to see the Old Man of the Mountains, the striking rock profile that Nathaniel Hawthorne had made famous in "The Great Stone Face." On another, they walked to Echo Lake, testing the echo by shouting, *"Freedom everywhere, slavery nowhere."* Their words bounced back at them. So did a spoiled egg that some men tossed a moment later.

In her letters Lucretia described the waterfalls and wild ravines, the Indian wigwams where she bought sweet-smell-

ing baskets, and the "too-good living" at the hotel. "Aunt
Elizabeth is growing quite fat and your mother has gained
also."

But before the vacation ended she was beginning to fret.
"I shall have lots to do at home to pay for all this dissipa-
tion."

On the return trip she attended a string of meetings in
Boston, Providence, and Worcester, sometimes speaking at
two in one day. By the time she reached Philadelphia she
was almost as thin and tense as when she had left.

Realizing that a more radical change was necessary,
James and the children held a series of family conclaves.
Reluctantly they concluded that the only way to protect
Lucretia from constant demands on her time was to sell
338 and move to the country. After looking around, James
settled on a small farmhouse on Old York Road, eight miles
north of Philadelphia and just across the way from Oak
Farm.

Roadside, as the Motts named their new home, was an
old-fashioned stone house that had been built in Colonial
times. For almost a year, carpenters and masons remodeled
the building, adding two roomy wings as well as a furnace
in the cellar and a shower bath. While James took charge
of the orchard and garden, Lucretia haunted secondhand
shops to find sofas and corner cupboards for the new house.
During the final weeks before the move, James made daily
trips to the country with wagonloads of furniture. Lucretia
went along to lay carpets and oversee the painters—"and
occasionally lend a hand until an old horse is limber com-
pared with thy sister," she told Martha.

Then it was time for the last family gathering on Arch
Street. As Lucretia walked through the rooms, stripped of
their familiar furnishings, she had doubts about the wisdom

of her self-exile. Echoing her mood, children and grand-children wrote a series of "poems of lamentation" for the occasion:

> Who wearied of the world's renown,
> And sought a useful life to crown,
> By selling off his house in town?
>   James Mott.
> Who was it that the sale decreed,
> And urged him on to do the deed,
> And wished to close the terms with speed?
>   Lucretia.
> Who constantly will ring the bell,
> And ask if they will please to tell
> Where Mrs. Mott has gone to dwell?
>   The beggars.
> Who never, never, never more
> Will see the 'lions' at the door
> That they've so often seen before?
>   The neighbors.
> And who will miss, for months at least,
> That place of rest for man and beast,
> From North and South and West and East?
>   Everybody.

When they ended with:

> Weep for the glory of Three-thirty-eight!
> Weep for the family, once so elate!
> Weep for the friends who their sorrows will date
> From the day of the closing of 338!

there was scarcely anyone in the room whose eyes were not filled with tears.

24. Roadside

No part of this—our country home—is more novel to
me than to feel that Time is mine to do as I list.
LUCRETIA MOTT, 1857

It was spring when the Motts moved to Roadside. "The
bushes and trees are putting on their most inviting green.
The wrens are building their nests and the robins beginning to be heard," Lucretia wrote Martha. "You ought to
have heard our children laugh at their mother for prais-
ing up these country delights."

She continued to praise the country delights. She took
long walks with Watch, their dog, who was "homely but
such a staunch barker." She enjoyed the thrifty feeling of
baking pies with cherries from her own trees and puddings
from her own milk and eggs. She liked the sound of the
mowing machines in summer, and the fragrance of the new-
cut hay that drifted in through the open windows. The
open windows also brought flies—and these she pursued as
relentlessly as if they were enemies of reform.

When the Davis' cat had so many litters that Oak Farm
and Roadside were overrun with kittens, only Lucretia had
the courage to do what country people always did with un-
wanted animals—drown them.

"Oh, Mother, how could you?" Patty asked.

"My destructiveness has been so exercised in killing flies
that I'm ready for anything but humans," Lucretia joked.
"Besides"—she turned on James and George Lord who also
looked reproachful—"you don't hesitate to butcher the pigs

or rob the poor cow of her calf for your convenience. I can't see why you should have a morbid tenderness for kittens."

Despite Roadside's new satisfactions, Lucretia was in no danger of becoming countrified. In addition to Oak Farm and The Hut, a summer house that the Cavenders had bought, other friends lived in the neighborhood. The Hallowells, who were active abolitionists, were just down the road, and the Yales, a family from New York State, had a place near them. Linus Yale, Lucretia reported to Martha, was the inventor of a lock that couldn't be picked.

On First days, the Motts drove to meeting at Germantown. On Sixth day evenings, they walked two miles to Shoemakertown, where a group of local people had organized a debating society to discuss such questions as "Is war under any circumstances justifiable?" or "Are the Garrisonian Abolitionists entitled to the support of the American people?" The leader of this group was Robert Collyer, a young Englishman who made claw hammers in a nearby forge and preached in the Methodist church on Sundays. When he criticized the Garrisonians, Lucretia answered him. At the conclusion of her speech, the blacksmith threw up his hands.

"You are right," he apologized. "I will fight henceforth under your banner."

After this encounter, James invited him to visit. Ruddy-faced Collyer, who still spoke with a marked Yorkshire accent, accepted the invitation doubtfully. To him, the Motts represented the upper class, and he was determined not to be patronized. A few minutes in their parlor were enough to reassure him. "It was simply like going into another and ampler home of my own," he later wrote.

In the stimulating atmosphere of Roadside, the young

workingman blossomed. Although he had had only two years of formal schooling, he was hungry for the kind of books and ideas he found at the Motts'. Night after night he dropped in to read a *History of Civilization* with Edward Davis or to compare notes on a lecture of Emerson's with Lucretia. A natural orator, he was quick to join the ranks of anti-slavery speakers. But as he began to travel throughout the state preaching abolition, the elders of his church objected. Torn between his love for his church and the more liberal ideas he had been encountering, he turned to Lucretia for guidance.

Sympathetic with his struggle, she told him of the unhappy period of the Quaker separation, when she faced the reproaches of old friends in order, as she said, "to be true to my own soul." From these conversations with Lucretia, Robert Collyer found the strength to break with his whole way of life. Leaving his job at the hammer factory, he accepted the pastorate of a Unitarian church in the West. In subsequent years, he became one of the country's leading clergymen and public speakers.

After her first summer at Roadside, Lucretia went to Philadelphia once or twice each week. When Wendell Phillips lectured, she stayed at Tom's overnight in order to hear him. The following morning she brought Wendell home with her for a day in the country.

Ordinarily James drove her to the city in their dearborn, a square covered wagon with an inexhaustible capacity for the chickens, eggs, and vegetables that she insisted on bringing to family and friends. When she traveled on the steam cars, she never went emptyhanded, even if it meant carrying two or three freshly laid eggs in her handbag. Nor did she fail to buy a cake or trifling gift for her grandchildren on the return trip.

On her way home one afternoon, she spotted a high chair in her favorite secondhand store. The chair was just right for Ellen Lord, Patty's two-year-old, and she had it delivered to the cars. When she reached her stop, the conductor carried it to the little open shed that served as station. Contrary to custom, no one was waiting to meet her. With scarcely a second thought, sixty-four-year-old Lucretia took off her bonnet and put the chair upside-down on her head. Balancing it with one hand, she proceeded slowly across the fields to the house.

"It's not heavy!" she protested when Patty, glimpsing her from a window, ran out to take it.

The first years at Roadside were ones of mounting tension throughout the country. A business depression had again thrown thousands out of work and even the Motts began to feel "a pocket-cramp." Tom went to England and France, seeking new markets for their firm's woolens, while Maria and Edward moved to Roadside for the winter to save fuel.

"Our children are all economizing in every way—renewing old clothes, making their own bonnets and lots of other things," Lucretia told Martha. "As to my apparel, it has never been other than mean, so I can make no change."

Overshadowing the money panic was the dark specter of civil war. David Wright had gone to Kansas, bringing rifles to the settlers who were fighting to keep the territory a free state. James's brother, Richard, a Congressman from Ohio, was one of the founders of the new Republican party. He wrote from Washington to tell them of the brutal beating of Charles Sumner. After speaking on "The Crime Against Kansas," Sumner had been beaten into insensibility on the Senate floor by a Congressman from South Carolina. When he visited the Motts three months later, Sumner still walked with a tottering step.

"His presence excited all the young 'uns," Lucretia said.

Young and old continued to be excited as the conflict came closer and closer. When the Pennsylvania Anti-Slavery Society met in October 1859, the familiar speeches on free produce and the slave trade seemed out-of-date. As president of the society, white-haired James Mott greeted the delegates with a solemn statement, "We meet to abolish slavery!"

It was Robert Purvis, however, who expressed the new feeling of urgency. Attacking those Americans who professed to believe in freedom while holding four million slaves in bondage, he said, "I welcome the bolt, whether coming from heaven or hell, that should shiver the American Union to pieces!"

Days later the bolt struck. The Motts were hurrying home from the convention to get Roadside ready for its first wedding—their granddaughter Anna Davis's marriage to Richard Hallowell—when John Brown and twenty-one followers captured the government arsenal at Harpers Ferry, Virginia. After seizing guns and ammunition, Brown planned to lead a guerrilla army through the South, freeing the slaves.

His plan failed. Facing the armed might of the United States, most of his band, including two of his sons, were killed and he was thrown into a Virginia jail. But his daring deed served to awaken the nation as no speech had ever done. For six weeks, until he was hanged for high treason, Northerners and Southerners debated furiously.

Was Brown a madman, a murderer? Or was he, as Emerson said, "That new saint who will make the gallows glorious like the cross?"

Throughout their lives, the Motts opposed force and violence. In the panicky period following the raid when the press held the abolitionists responsible for the bloodshed, they might easily have remained in seclusion at Roadside. Instead, they came to Philadelphia every day to urge support for Brown and his family. At a meeting at Concert Hall when Congressman Joshua R. Giddings of Ohio said, "If I were a slave I would walk over the dead bodies of my enslavers from Mississippi to Malden," James sat at Giddings' side, approving not the war principles that the speaker advocated, but the bravery of the man who dared to make them.

During Brown's trial, Miller McKim escorted Mrs. Brown to Virginia for a farewell meeting with her husband. While she waited in Philadelphia for permission for the visit, she spent several days at Roadside. Admiring her courage, Lucretia and her daughters attempted to comfort her.

"I am happy that you are under Mrs. Mott's roof," Brown wrote in one of his last letters. "I remember the faithful old lady well, but presume she has no recollection of me. I am glad to have you make the acquaintance of such old pioneers in the cause."

On the day of Brown's execution, the McKims and young Richard Hallowell undertook the melancholy task of bringing his body to his home in the Adirondacks for burial. In Philadelphia, the abolitionists held a memorial prayer meeting in his honor. With James Mott presiding, Lucretia was a principal speaker.

"I am no preacher of the milk-and-water passive spirit of non-resistance to wrong," she explained. "Robert Purvis has said that I was the most belligerent non-resistant he ever saw. I accept the character he gives me and glory in it. I have no idea of submitting tamely to injustice inflicted either on me or on the slave. I will oppose it with all the moral powers with which I am endowed.

"Quakerism, as I understand it, does not mean quietism. The early Friends were agitators, disturbers of the peace, and were more obnoxious in their day than we are."

While this tiny disturber of the peace defended John Brown, Philadelphia was in a turmoil. Two hundred medical students marched from the city in a body to offer their services to Virginia's governor. Prominent merchants held a meeting to conciliate the South, hoping that "the ravings of a few half-insane fanatics" would not be mistaken for the sentiments of Philadelphians.

In this atmosphere, the Anti-Slavery Fair opened its doors in the spacious saloon of Concert Hall. To advertise the sale, the Fair Committee had prepared a flag with a picture of the Liberty Bell and its inscription, "Proclaim liberty throughout all the land unto all the inhabitants thereof." Suspended across Chestnut Street, the flag vied for attention with a banner advertising a life-size painting of Venus.

To the surprise of the exhibitor of the half-nude painting, the Liberty Bell drew larger crowds than Venus. In a few hours, the mayor ordered the Fair flag taken down. Its motto, he said, was an incitement to riot. As crowds continued to congregate outside the hall, the sheriff appeared. Armed with a writ, he locked the doors of the saloon and gave the women three hours to pack.

Replying to his polite expression of regret, Lucretia was steely eyed. "We don't reproach thee for thy part in this affair," she assured him. "We are sorry for thee, because thou holds an office which obliges thee to perform such deeds."

With a team of willing helpers, the committee moved its

wares to the Assembly Buildings. By the following day, they were back in business. Despite continual threats, Anna Hopper, the Fair treasurer, was able to announce receipts of $2087.

In the fall of 1860, another banner stretched across Chestnut Street: *CONCESSION BEFORE SECESSION.* By then, however, it was too late for concession. Abraham Lincoln was elected in November, winning a majority even in Philadelphia. While the Female Anti-Slavery Society held its 25th annual Fair, South Carolina seceded from the Union.

25. James and Self

I owe the happiness of my own wedded life to the fact that my husband and I have always shared a deep interest in the sacred cause of wronged humanity.

LUCRETIA MOTT

Two days before Confederate troops fired on Fort Sumter, a simple hand-written invitation brought several hundred people to Roadside:

James and Lucretia Mott
At Home
4th month, 10th, 1861
From 3 to 7 o'clock P.M.
Golden Wedding

Grandchildren and one tiny great grandchild romped on the lawn and played croquet while older guests signed their names to a testimonial on the back of the Motts' wedding certificate. After the ceremony was over, Anna Hopper couldn't restrain her curiosity.

"Mother," she asked, "what happened to thy certificate? Why is the bottom corner cut away?"

Lucretia glanced at the parchment scroll, yellowed with age. Should she destroy the solemnity of the occasion by telling the story? The corners of her mouth twitched. "Thou dost not remember? Thou wert playing battledore and shuttlecock when we lived on Union Street. Thy battledore tore and thou set up such a wail that I mended it with the first piece of parchment that came to hand—our wedding certificate!"

James laughed along with the rest of the company. Despite her gray hair and the wrinkles etching her broad forehead, how little Lucretia had changed since he first saw her across the playground fence at Nine Partners. Although years of self-discipline had curbed her impatience, she was still impulsive, still a "long tongue" who could run rings around him in debate.

He chuckled as he recalled a recent dinner table conversation. Speaking of a homesick young bride, he had remarked that the Bible said that a woman must leave father and mother and cleave to her husband.

Lucretia's brows knitted. "Where dost thou find that description, my dear?" she asked in a dangerously calm voice.

"Well, what is it then?" he sighed, realizing that he was about to be bested.

"If thou will check thy Scriptures, thou will find that it is the *man* who shall leave father and mother and cleave unto his wife."

In their half-century together, James had scarcely changed either. Years as president of the Pennsylvania Anti-Slavery Society and as a leader in other reform groups had given him self-assurance, but he still retained traces of his youthful modesty. Aware that he was not as well known as his wife, he tried to remain in the background. On a Western trip, when asked to sign an Anti-Slavery Register, he wrote in his characteristic, self-effacing style, *"I am an old, plain, matter-of-fact man, not given to sentiment, but if my autograph is wanted in addition to that of my better half, here it is."*

Although Lucretia teased him about his reticence, she was the first to appreciate the qualities that lay behind it.

She liked to tell of the time his brother, Richard, who was almost James's counterpart, was visiting. When she walked into the parlor, she found the two men sitting side by side, "in perfect silence."

"I thought you must both be here," she said. "It was so still!"

On another occasion, after returning from a trip, she wrote Martha, "James has been remarkably bearing in the absence of buttons—being of as few words in such a catastrophe as is his wont in others in the miseries of life. The most striking evidence of dissatisfaction is in finding the buttonless shirt thrown on the bed and another put on in its place."

It was not only in the matter of buttons that James was "bearing." Over the years, the differences in their personalities had served to bind them closer together. As she dashed ahead, sometimes battering herself against stone walls in her crusades, he was the slow, steady balance wheel that gave her the strength to go on. In large things and small, he tried to lift responsibilities from her frail shoulders.

Often, when she was overwhelmed by her correspondence, James tackled the stack of unanswered letters. Even then Lucretia couldn't refrain from looking over his shoulder and inserting a word here and there. Nathaniel Barney saved one letter which was almost a running dialogue between the two. While James described Lucretia's busy life, she added parenthetical comments:

"She has numerous calls almost daily of all sorts of folks, high and low, rich and poor, for advice, assistance, encouragement. (*Rather exaggerated*) I am sometimes around to hear the object of some of the callers—it seems as though some thought she could do anything and everything and it is true that she does a great deal. (*Quite a mistake*). I could say a great deal more (*far too much already for a partial eulogist*) truly too of my dear Lucretia but she will not like what I have said. (*that's a fact*) She dislikes to see anything of herself in print unless it is in the way of condemnation and that she does not care about. (*That is a mistake too for she don't relish blame any better than any of her neighbors.*) . . ."

Although James took over some of her correspondence, Lucretia continued to write the gossipy family sheets. As her children and grandchildren moved to different parts of the world she routed these letters from Auburn to New York and from Boston to London as if she were dispatching trains at a busy railroad terminus. Poking fun at her efficiency, Tom ended a business letter to Edward Hopper with a warning: "Don't let Mother send this to Nantucket."

"They may make as much fun as they please," Lucretia sniffed. "I know what I am about."

She sometimes complained that her outlay for stamps for the bulky family letters amounted to ninety cents. Fortunately, she no longer had worries about postage. In spite of ups and downs, James had become a successful merchant. Before their move to Roadside, he was able to turn over his business to Tom and retire with a substantial income.

At Roadside, he continued to supervise additions to the house and farm. His family was delighted when he installed a water closet, one of the first of its kind in the neighborhood. "We are to have a convenience in the downstairs bathroom," Lucretia wrote Anna Brown. "Won't it be nice?" And then, because she was always conscience-stricken about wasting money, she added, "The place will sell all the better."

Even when they were prosperous, the Motts never forgot their early habits of thrift. They still kept an accurate record of expenditures, believing that carelessness with money was close to a crime. Lucretia particularly objected to wasting paper. Paper, made from linen rags and not from wood pulp as it is now, was expensive. She wrote in a tiny, neat script, finishing in the margins or writing between the lines to avoid starting a fresh sheet.

In her youth, envelopes were unheard-of. Instead, letters were folded over and sealed with a drop of wax. After envelopes came into general use, she saved those that she received. Cutting them open carefully, she made notes on their blank insides or gave them to her great-grandchildren to scribble on.

Although they kept track of pennies, Lucretia and James gave away a large portion of their income. The tenants of the "beggars' chairs" at 338 quickly found their way to Roadside—and seldom left emptyhanded. Lucretia wrote in one letter, "My purse was opening for a quarter when James drew out a dollar and handed her—I've often found he was more generous than his wife."

After James's retirement, she filled her letters with reports of "James and self." When she had meetings to go to in Pennsylvania or New Jersey, he drove her in their dearborn. Despite their advancing age, bad weather rarely bothered them. In winter they kept a hot-water box at their feet and what Lucretia described as a "cat buffalo robe" tucked around their knees. In summer the roof of the dearborn was sufficient protection against sudden showers. The year after their golden wedding anniversary, they drove all the way to Auburn. Lucretia stopped to visit Martha, but James went on to Buffalo to show Anna and Maria Niagara Falls.

Jogging along on these trips with the reins in his lap, James was content to watch the changing landscape while Lucretia knitted and talked. She had always liked quilts and table covers made of marseilles, a thick cotton cloth with a raised design. Formerly she had been able to purchase English marseilles manufactured from "free" cotton. When this was no longer available, she bought yarn at the Free Produce Store and made the cloth herself. Knitting little pieces in the form of stars or shells, she sewed them together on her return home. In this way she was able to supply not only Roadside, but the households of her children and grandchildren as well.

When they were at home, Lucretia and James spent the early hours of the day in their library, a quiet retreat away from the noisy dining room and parlor. The library was a small book-lined room with a glass door opening onto the piazza. Its walls were decorated with portraits of Elias Hicks, William Lloyd Garrison, Robert Purvis, and other old friends, along with a map of Nantucket and a genealogical chart of the Coffin family.

Lucretia's two-shelfed table stood next to her rocking chair, its upper surface covered with books and writing materials, its lower given over to sewing baskets. When she enjoyed a book, she liked to read the best parts of it aloud. If James was in the garden and she couldn't buttonhole any of her children, she made notes on cut-open envelopes and stowed them away for later reference.

James was less of a serious reader than she, but when he was absorbed in a book he couldn't put it down. His grandchildren remembered him sitting in his straight-backed chair near the fire with a new book in his lap. When dusk came, he was still reading. The gas was lighted earlier than usual, so that he might continue. At bedtime he was

still absorbed and at breakfast the next morning he refused
to tell at what hour of the night he had stopped. The magi-
cal book was *Uncle Tom's Cabin*—and even Lucretia listened to an occasional chapter.

When Harriet Beecher Stowe came to Philadelphia,
"James and self" drove her and her twin daughters to
Frankford where there was a mental hospital that she was
interested in seeing. Lucretia thought that Mrs. Stowe was
"handsomer than was expected" with a diffident but pleas-
ing manner.

As James grew older, his eyesight begain to fail. His
bright-eyed wife found it "really affecting" when he put
down a book and sighed, "I can't see to read." She kept
him abreast of the family letters, while his children read to
him from the current books and magazines. In this way
Lucretia, too, became acquainted with the poems of Ten-
nyson and Browning and Dickens' latest novels.

When Edward Everett Hale's story, *The Man Without a
Country*, appeared in *The Atlantic Monthly*, she told Martha, "The moral is good and it is very well told, but made-up
stories cannot interest me as plain matters of fact do. Still,
I always like to be told what is worth reading in the peri-
odicals. I couldn't be hired to go over all the trash, but
Edward and Maria make nice selections to read aloud."

James who had always dreamed of becoming a farmer
spent much of his time in the fields and barn. He bought
prize pigs from Robert Purvis and smoked the hams himself, while Patty helped Lucretia prepare sausage and
scrapple from the leftovers. From spring until fall, he was
seldom without a long-handled weed cutter with which he
jabbed at the roots of crab grass or plaintain as he walked
around the grounds. The youngsters who followed him—
great-grandchildren now—collected the weeds in little piles

and begged for a story when he sat down to rest in the shade of a pear tree near the house.

His fondness for children and theirs for him led him to take an increasing interest in education. One of his pet projects was the "establishment of a Board School for Friends' Children and for the Education of Teachers." He traveled to neighboring communities to talk to groups of boys and girls about the school that eventually became Swarthmore College.

In accordance with Quaker custom, the Motts were frequently asked to be witnesses at Friends' weddings, "to see that good order is observed." To numerous young couples, James, with his white hair worn long in the style of his youth and Lucretia in her old-fashioned cap and dress, seemed to symbolize a happy married life. After keeping a sharp ear cocked for the language of the ceremony, for she disliked to hear a bride promise to "obey," Lucretia gave a few words of advice. In her later years, she wrote out her prescription for success in marriage and gave a copy to each bridal pair:

"In the true marriage relation the independence of the husband and wife is equal, their dependence mutual and their obligations reciprocal."

26. The Day of Jubilee

The great job is ended. The occasion is one of con-
gratulation, and I cannot but congratulate all pres-
ent, myself, the country, and the whole world upon
this great moral victory!

ABRAHAM LINCOLN, 1865

The Motts greeted the beginning of the Civil War with mixed emotions. Accepting the Quaker testimony for peace, Lucretia believed it wrong to fight except with moral weapons. When they were first married, James had spent two days in the Arch Street jail for refusing militia service. Yet now most of the young men she knew—Quakers, non-resistants—were putting aside principles to join the army.

Her first shock came when Edward Davis appeared in the library wearing the blue uniform and epaulets of a Union officer. Edward who had always deplored the barbarous resort to war, Edward who had worked with her to make converts to the peace movement . . .

"I know what they will say, Mother." He tried to forestall her objections. "However, I have been talking to both General Frémont and the President. This must not get abroad yet, but the general showed me an order he plans to issue freeing the slaves in the Department of the West. Freeing the slaves!"

"And thou, Edward," Lucretia asked. "Thou flatter thyself that the abolition of slavery end justifies the means?"

She felt sick at heart when Edward went to St. Louis to join Frémont's staff. She felt sicker still when Frémont did issue his emancipation order, and Lincoln promptly countermanded it.

Lincoln's actions in succeeding months only confirmed her lifelong distrust of politicians. Peppering her letters with comments on "our imbecile President," she urged everyone to petition Washington—"so that poor Abe, McClellan, and the others may see how unavailing all their pro-slavery conservatism is."

During 1862, her point of view began to change. Although she still believed that war was wrong and did all that she could to support the small group of Friends whose consciences wouldn't permit them to bear arms, she followed the news with breathless interest.

"Can you read anything but the papers?" she asked Martha.

First came the abolition of slavery in the District of Columbia. Then, on the heels of a War Department order to enlist blacks as soldiers, the President issued his preliminary Emancipation Proclamation. Lucretia wasn't won over entirely. The proclamation offered freedom only in the future, besides failing to provide for the slaves in the loyal border states.

"But if it's properly carried out, a bright prospect is opening before us. Lincoln has done well *for him,*" she grudgingly admitted.

On her seventieth birthday, Lucretia and James drove along snowy roads to meet with the Female Anti-Slavery Society. The President had signed the final Emancipation Proclamation. After all the years of meetings, all the speeches and resolutions, all the signatures so painstakingly collected on petitions, freedom was near!

Her gray eyes dancing, Lucretia proposed a resolution:

"We hail with unutterable joy and gratitude the day of Jubilee which has dawned on the American nation."

Freedom was near, but there was still a long hard war to be won. At Roadside, scarcely a day passed without the arrival of a young recruit on his way to join his regiment— Willie Wright, the Garrison and Hallowell boys, Charlie Purvis who was one of the Army's first Negro surgeons. Bearded and travel-stained, the boys bathed and slept, and hungrily devoured the puddings that Lucretia set before them.

When the boys came, so did the girls. Although Lucretia steadily refused to find the soldiers' uniforms glamorous —"it seems childish for men grown to rig out in that style" —she looked on complacently when the young people crowded into the parlor for a game of Authors or gave an evening party on the lawn. For once she had her fill of matchmaking, as Ellen Wright paired off with Willie Garrison and Lucy McKim with his younger brother Wendell.

After Union forces captured a small area on the coast of South Carolina, Miller McKim went South to help distribute land and establish schools there. Accompanying her father on several occasions, Lucy brought back some extraordinary songs composed by the Negroes. When she sang them at Roadside, even her tone-deaf hostess thought them "very touching." Lucy's collection of *Slave Songs of the United States*, published after the war, was the North's first introduction to Negro spirituals.

Despite these pleasant interludes, the war was not all music and romance. Early in the summer of 1863, General Lee crossed into Pennsylvania with eighty thousand men. Anticipating an attack, the mayor of Philadelphia organized an emergency home guard. Merchants doffed their broadcloth coats to dig trenches at the approaches to the city, while a silent crowd gathered on the State House lawn, waiting.

On the Fourth of July, rumors trickled in of a bloody battle at Gettysburg, a hundred miles away. The following day the rumors were confirmed and Philadelphians sighed with relief as the tattered remnants of Lee's army retreated to Virginia.

Maria was reading the *Tribune* aloud to her father the next day when she broke off with a cry. Close to the bottom of the long list of casualties at Gettysburg was a familiar name—"Lieutenant William P. Wright, aged 21." David Wright, pale with anxiety, arrived from Auburn soon afterward. Among the tens of thousands of wounded, there was no way of learning whether Willie was alive or dead without going to the battlefield.

Lucretia's offer to accompany him was immediately vetoed by her family, but Mariana, leaving her children at Roadside, went in her stead. The rickety, overcrowded train broke down. In the merciless summer sun, David and his stepdaughter walked miles along dusty roads to the military hospital. Willie wasn't in the hospital.

With sinking hearts, they crisscrossed the battlefield for another twenty-four hours. Stumbling into shell holes and turning away from the carcasses of cavalry horses, they at last found Willie in an attic room in a farmhouse, with a bullet hole through his chest.

Too weak to be moved, he remained in Gettysburg for a month before he was brought on a stretcher to Roadside. While his sisters and brothers took turns nursing him, his Aunt Lucretia said, "I pray for his preservation even while knowing I have no right to ask special favors."

Willie was not the only soldier Lucretia prayed for that summer. Two weeks after the Battle of Gettysburg, the

Massachusetts 54th saw action in South Carolina. The 54th, the first black regiment from the North, was the pride of the abolitionists. Its ranks included the sons of many old friends. As the regiment stormed the ramparts of Fort Wagner in Charleston harbor, its colonel, Robert Gould Shaw, and more than two hundred of his soldiers were killed. Mourning Shaw's death—"we all feel it very much" —Lucretia worried about the fate of Ned Hallowell, her neighbor's son. Wounded in the battle, Ned returned to the front after a brief rest at home, to command the 54th for the duration of the war.

In the next anxious months, Lucretia found herself absorbed in the affairs of Camp William Penn where Pennsylvania's colored troops received their basic training. Located less than a mile from Roadside, the camp became almost an annex of the Motts' household. Lucretia spoke there on First days and brought officers and men back home for tea.

These were her boys, no less than Willie and Ned. While James gave them money for a regimental flag, she supplied them with home-baked pies and baskets of peaches and apples. Discovering that the soldiers lacked a comfortable day room to use when off duty, she arranged for the settees belonging to the Female Anti-Slavery Society to be loaned to the camp for the duration.

When the black regiments completed their training and left for the South, it became their custom to march through the back gate of Roadside and out at the front, in order to wave goodbye to the Motts. As soon as she heard them approach, Lucretia would empty the contents of the cake box in her apron. Stationing herself at the end of the piazza, she leaned over the railing and gave each man a piece of gingerbread as he passed.

In spite of her dislike of military trappings she was as excited as the children when the camp band played the John Brown song and the black soldiers paraded down Old York Road in their trim blue uniforms.

"Is not this change in feeling towards this oppressed class beyond all that we could have anticipated, and marvelous in our eyes?" she wrote Martha.

As Union armies marched through the South, thousands and thousands of slaves left the plantations to declare themselves free. The abolitionists took the lead in finding food and shelter for them. In Philadelphia, Lucretia helped organize a Freedmen's Relief Association. Not only anti-slavery women, but conservative Friends who had avoided her for years came to Roadside to knit stockings and remodel clothing for the ex-slaves. Amused to find that she had become respectable, she wryly welcomed "these devoted friends even at the eleventh hour."

For the first time in a quarter of a century, there was no Anti-Slavery Fair in 1864. Instead, the Freedmen's Relief Association raised money to send teachers to liberated areas in the South. By the end of the year they were able to ship an entire schoolhouse, bell and all, to South Carolina. One of the first young lady teachers at this transplanted Penn School was James Forten's granddaughter, Charlotte.

In the last year of the war, Lucretia was on the go all the time. After traveling to Auburn in the fall for Ellen Wright's wedding to Willie Garrison, she spent three or four days each week in Philadelphia. By the time her seventy-second birthday rolled around, she was feeling so poorly that she left a roomful of well-wishers and retired to the library. Miller McKim found her there, suffering from severe dyspeptic pains.

Under his prodding, she counted up the number of

freedmen's aid meetings, social gatherings, weddings, and funerals that she had attended in the preceding month. When he discovered that every day had been occupied, he diagnosed her ailment as "mental and moral over-work." Sheepishly, she agreed to take some rest.

"It really makes me feel old to see how they won't let me do anything," she was soon complaining. "I was making our bed when Patty came and forced me away, just as if I was not far better able than she to stir around. When people treat me as if I had one foot in the grave, I feel disposed to say—'No, you don't!'"

After all, how could a body rest, when so much was happening? While Congress debated a Thirteenth Amendment to the Constitution, an amendment that would outlaw slavery in every section of the country, Sherman's men were heading North from Georgia. Charleston fell, then Peterboro, then Richmond.

During the night of April 9, Lucretia was awakened by a chorus of bells. From the State House all the way to Germantown every church and firehouse bell was ringing. As she looked out of her window she could see bonfires and torchlight processions. General Lee had surrendered. The hateful war was over and the slaves were free!

Only six days later, the headlines leaped out at her from the morning paper:

AWFUL EVENT
PRESIDENT LINCOLN
SHOT BY AN
ASSASSIN

She was so stunned that she could hardly go on with her housework. That afternoon the bells rang again. This time they were tolling a funeral dirge.

"Such a display of mourning as now in the city was never before," she wrote Martha. "All business suspended, men crying in the streets. The children have festooned drapery the length of our piazza. I objected at first, but finding that Edward D. had brought out a quantity of black muslin and wished much to do it, I didn't care.

"A beautiful day! When a real calamity is over the nation you want the sun to be darkened and the moon not to give her light. But how everything goes on, just as if such an awful thing had not happened. Was there ever such universal sorrow?"

27. The Postwar World

When the true history of the anti-slavery cause shall be written, women will occupy a large space in its pages; for the cause of the slave has been peculiarly women's cause. Foremost among those noble American women, in point of clearness of vision, breadth of understanding, fullness of knowledge, catholicity of spirit, weight of character, and widespread influence was Lucretia Mott.

FREDERICK DOUGLASS

William Lloyd Garrison arrived at Roadside in a jubilant mood. He had been to South Carolina as a guest of the government, to witness the return of the United States flag to Fort Sumter. Afterward, freedmen carried him in triumph on their shoulders, presenting him with so many flowers that a companion said, "You began your warfare in the face of rotten eggs and brickbats. Behold, you end it on a bed of roses!"

"Our thirty-five-year-long war is over," he exulted as a group gathered around the fireplace in the library. "Slavery is abolished and so is anti-slavery. We are out of work, thank God!"

Robert Purvis disagreed. "Our work won't be done until every freedman has the ballot. Without it, they are at the mercy of their former masters. Prejudice against color is as strong as ever, even in the North."

"Prejudice—colorphobia—is a product of the slave system," Garrison argued. "With the abolition of slavery, it will quickly disappear."

As she pushed the chairs in a sociable circle around the fire, stepping on vagrant sparks that threatened her carpet, Lucretia wondered which of the two was right. She was still thinking about the discussion when she rode in to Philadelphia the following week. Sitting in a horse car, she noticed a black woman climb aboard. After collecting her fare, the conductor motioned her to the front platform. It was beginning to rain, and the woman pulled her shawl over her head before she reluctantly obeyed.

Lucretia's knitting bag closed with a snap. In a moment she was at the conductor's elbow. "In this weather," she suggested, "thou could let her ride inside. She—"

"Can't, ma'am." The conductor cut her off. "My order is 'Colored out on the platform.' I don't make the rules."

"Perhaps thou dost not make the rules, but thou could break them," Lucretia flared.

"Orders is orders." When he indicated by a shrug of his shoulders that the subject was closed, Lucretia marched outside to stand next to the colored woman. As the door closed behind her, the passengers exchanged uneasy glances. Thin little Lucretia who was all eyes and chin looked even older than her seventy-two years—and the rain was now coming down in sheets.

"She'll catch her death," one woman scolded.

Again the conductor shrugged. "T'ain't my concern," he pointed out. "I told the colored woman to go out, not *her.*"

As the downpour grew worse and other passengers began to murmur, he opened the front window. "Lady, you better come back in here."

Lucretia looked up at him in surprise. "I see thou dost not understand. I cannot go in without this woman."

The perplexed conductor stared at her for a moment. Resignedly he said, "Oh well, bring her in then."

With a satisfied nod, Lucretia led her companion back inside the car. Wiping the raindrops from her cheeks, she again opened her knitting bag.

Outwardly calm, she was seething inwardly. She continued to seethe until the next meeting of the Female Anti-Slavery Society. Then she proposed a resolution—"That this society do something to awaken the public against this most unjust and cruel treatment of our colored people."

Over the next two years, the Female Society petitioned the directors of the street railway companies, boycotted the cars, and joined with other groups in holding protest meetings. At last, in 1867, the Pennsylvania legislature passed a law forbidding discrimination in public transportation.

The incident on the horse car convinced Lucretia that the abolitionists had to continue with their work. If Negroes in Philadelphia were not permitted to ride inside the cars— or to vote in the city elections, or to send their children to integrated schools—how much worse the situation in the South must be. When Garrison resigned from the Anti-Slavery Society and closed down *The Liberator* at the end of the year, she sided with Wendell Phillips who became president of the society.

Garrison was not the only one who disagreed with his friends about the future. Sometimes it seemed as if everyone Lucretia knew had his own blueprint for the postwar world. Miller McKim wanted the anti-slavery and freedmen's aid societies to merge into a broad Union Association. Men who had always shied away from the abolitionists were promising him financial support for *The Nation*, a new paper that he and his son-in-law, Wendell Garrison, were starting. Although *The Nation* was to be a weekly of news and opinion, it would speak for the Union Association and keep a watchful eye on freedmen's problems. He had gotten around to asking James to buy stock in the magazine when Lucretia interrupted.

"Thou has ignored the women in thy new organization," she pointed out. "If there is to be a real reconstruction of the nation, it will be rather a comedown for the anti-slavery and Quaker women to be overlooked."

Miller was taken aback. For four years nothing had been heard from the woman's right leaders. In the interest of unity, they had refrained from calling conventions. Instead they had poured their energies into a Loyal League which supported the war and the cause of freedom for the slave.

"If there seems a necessity for women," Miller stammered, "I think they would be admitted."

"Seems a necessity!" Lucretia raised her eyebrows. "Seems a necessity for one-half the nation to act with you—and the larger half, I might say, with so many men slain."

McKim went away crestfallen. "You ought to have been here," Lucretia wrote Martha. "He couldn't ask James with quite so good a grace for $1000. He did ask, but I guess he will not get anything like so much."

During the summer of 1865, Lucretia and James shut their eyes to the world's problems for a time to consider problems of their own. Their daughter, Elizabeth, had come home to die. Pale and hollow-cheeked, she lay on the piazza through the long summer days. While James took her youngsters for walks, Lucretia busied herself with shawls and cups of nourishing broth. Hiding their heartache, the elderly couple watched Elizabeth linger on until fall. Lucretia was listless and despondent for many months afterward.

The following spring she and James went to New York for a week of conventions. The trip perked her up as no medicine had been able to do. Patty and George had moved to Brooklyn during the war. The Motts stayed with them, taking the cars to Manhattan each morning. Between convention sessions, Grandmother Lucretia read to Patty's children who had the measles. She also found time to buy pillow and bolster muslin at Stewart's Department Store. She was disappointed, however, because she never managed to darn Patty's stockings as she had planned!

Chairing the Woman's Rights meeting for a day, she supported their decision to form an Equal Rights Association to work for suffrage for all Americans, black as well as white, women as well as men. Despite her protest that "Age and feebleness unfit me for public duties," she was unanimously elected president of the new organization.

The Equal Rights Association began as a society of men and women, with Elizabeth Stanton and Frederick Douglass as vice-presidents. It quickly foundered on the shoals of practical politics. In the troubled years after the war, blacks in the South were in danger of being re-enslaved by their former masters. To protect their dearly-bought freedom, they needed the right to vote—and Congress was disposed to grant it to them.

When Elizabeth Stanton and her co-worker, Susan Anthony, discovered that the proposed Fourteenth and Fifteenth Amendments to the Constitution conferred citizenship only on men, they balked. If the Constitution was to be drastically amended, they saw a chance for woman suffrage that might not occur again for a long time.

"Do you believe the African race is composed entirely of males?" Elizabeth indignantly asked Wendell Phillips.

Phillips, who was no longer speaking to his old friend, Garrison, soon refused to shake Elizabeth Stanton's hand when they met at a friend's home. Lucretia Mott picked her way across the battlefield as judiciously as she could. As an abolitionist, she wanted the constitutional amendments adopted. As a woman, she thought that Elizabeth's insistence on universal suffrage was correct—although she did think Elizabeth was "too hard on Wendell."

In 1869 she presided over a stormy woman's suffrage meeting in Washington. Reporters scribbled furiously in their notebooks as Charles Purvis, who had become a doctor in the capital's Freedmen's Hospital, criticized the women's position and Robert Purvis defended it. Edward Davis then sided with Charles, and was answered by his mother-in-law—"with her usual gentleness," one newspaper said.

Martha Wright took the chair at the convention's evening session when Lucretia, aged 76, felt tired. *"Susan Anthony gave them fits,"* Martha wrote in her diary, *"and Sister L. poured on Balm of 1000 flowers."*

It was at this same convention that the chaplain of the Senate, Dr. Gray, opened the meeting with a prayer. Choosing as his text the second chapter of Genesis, he recounted the scene in the Garden of Eden when God made Eve, as an afterthought, out of one of Adam's ribs. Sitting on the platform next to Elizabeth Stanton, Lucretia stiffened.

"I cannot bow my head to such absurdities," she whispered.

From his seat in the auditorium, Edward Davis caught the bit of byplay on the platform. Biting his lip to keep from laughing at the expression on Lucretia's face, he left the hall to look for a Bible. Just as Dr. Gray was saying "Amen," Edward walked up to the rostrum, book in hand. He read the *first* chapter of Genesis, in which God created man and woman at the same time, giving them both dominion over the earth.

After he had commented on the allegorical nature of the Bible, Lucretia rose. Reproaching Dr. Gray, she explained the meaning of the Genesis chapter that Edward had read.

"It tells us of the eternal oneness and equality of man and woman, the union of the masculine and feminine elements which are like positive and negative magnetism and the centripetal and centrifugal forces in nature."

When a paper commented on the novelty of criticizing a prayer, particularly one offered by the Senate chaplain, Lucretia smiled mischievously. "If we can teach clergymen to be as careful what they say to God as to man, our conventions at the capital will be of great service to our representatives," she told Elizaeth.

Although she continued to support both black and woman suffrage, she was relieved when the breach between the men and women began to heal after the Fifteenth Amendment was ratified. With the Constitution guaranteeing full citizenship for the freedmen, the abolitionists decided that their goal had at last been reached. In 1870, Lucretia presided over the final meeting of the Female Anti-Slavery Society. "My heart is so full that there is room only for a feeling of thankfulness," she said. "Truly the Lord has triumphed gloriously."

28. A Light Goes Out

*How shall I describe to you Lucretia Mott—the most
brilliant eyes. Such a face and such regal erectness.
No one else ever stood upright before!*
THOMAS WENTWORTH HIGGINSON

In the first years after the war Lucretia and James were
often in Boston where their granddaughter, Anna Davis Hallowell, lived. In 1867 they attended the first meeting of the
Free Religious Association. Organized by men and women
of many faiths, including Emerson, Furness, and Rabbi
Isaac Wise of Cincinnati, the Association hoped to separate
genuine religious belief from the ceremonies and trappings
which too often weighed it down.

Several of the founders of the Free Religious Association
were also members of the Radical Club which met informally at the home of Reverend and Mrs. John T. Sargent
on Chestnut Street. The Radical Club brought together
New England's leading philosophers and writers, men like
Longfellow, the poet, and his minister brother, Samuel,
Oliver Wendell Holmes, Thomas Wentworth Higginson,
Henry James, as well as Emerson, Whittier, and Phillips.
Lucretia attended their meetings whenever she was in the
city, joining in the discussions on philosophy and listening
thoughtfully when scientific papers were read.

At one Radical Club meeting, Nathaniel Shaler, a Harvard geologist, gave a report on Charles Darwin's *Origin.
of Species.* Darwin's new theory of evolution which con-
tradicted the Biblical account of the Creation was under at-

tack in almost every church in the country. Harvard's Divinity School was in an uproar over it and even a zoology professor denounced the monstrous notion that man was descended from a monkey.

To the surprise of the younger members of the club, white-haired Lucretia, looking as if she had stepped from the eighteenth century, nodded vigorously as Shaler talked. When the floor was thrown open for discussion, she was the first to speak in Darwin's defense. "For the last fifty years I have been interested in the development of science," she explained. "I have learned to welcome it as a friend, not to fear it as a foe."

Telling Martha about the discussion afterward, she gleefully reported that she had been able to understand everything that Shaler said. "There were no hard words."

At another Radical Club session, the Motts were introduced to Lord and Lady Amberley, young English reformers who were touring the United States. Talking with them after the meeting Lucretia impulsively invited them to come home to dinner with her. With a sweep of her arm she managed to include several other people in the invitation.

While they were riding together on the train to Medford, the Boston suburb where the Hallowells lived, Lucretia was suddenly assailed by misgivings. How would her granddaughter who had four small children and no nursemaid react to the unexpected company?

At the Medford station, she hurried ahead to break the news. Half-dismayed and half-amused, she greeted Anna breathlessly. "What will thou say to me! I've asked Lord and Lady Amberley and William Lloyd Garrison out here to dine. And Aunt Martha and Willy are with them—and they are all just coming up the hill!"

The startled hostess had no chance to say anything, for

her guests were already at the door. She could only welcome them and follow the old Nantucket custom of adding extra potatoes to the chowder. To her surprise, it proved to be a delightful occasion with dinner followed by a memorable discussion of the position of women in America.

When the Amberleys visited Philadelphia a month later, they spent a day at Roadside. A warm friendship sprang up between the Motts and the titled young couple who named their first child Rachel Lucretia. "Your picture hangs up in my room," Lady Amberley wrote from England. "She shall be taught to venerate and love her far-off namesake whom I hope she may resemble."

In the summer of 1867, James and Lucretia took a long vacation, traveling to Nantucket and then to the Green Mountains. On their way home they stopped in Poughkeepsie. After a sentimental journey to Nine Partners, they toured Vassar College. Vassar, which had opened its doors two years earlier, was the first school in the East to offer a college-level education to girls. James was particularly interested in comparing it with Swarthmore which was scheduled to open soon.

This vacation was the last that the two spent together. On their way to New York the following winter, James caught a cold. Trifling at first, it developed into pneumonia. He died at Patty's home in Brooklyn, five months before his eightieth birthday.

Numbed by her loss, Lucretia let others make the funeral arrangements. The Lords brought her to Anna's house in Philadelphia. She sat dry-eyed through the funeral, scarcely hearing Robert Purvis' tribute—"I thank God for such a life!"—or noticing the group of black men who asked for the privilege of acting as pallbearers.

Back at Roadside, as letters of sympathy poured in from

all over the country and abroad, she wandered disconsolately from room to room. The library, the parlor, the bedroom—everything she saw reminded her of James. The big sunny bedroom seemed unbearably empty. She moved her belongings to a tiny room in the rear of the house where an east window permitted her to watch the sun rise.

"Oh, the great blank!" she mourned. "Scarcely a day passes that I do not think, of course for the instant only, that I will consult him about this or that."

Believing that "excessive grief is lamentable if not reprehensible," she gradually picked up the threads of her life again. Her children helped as much as they could. In addition to the Davises and Hoppers, Tom and Mariana hurried back from Europe to be with her, and Patty made frequent trips from New York.

The best tonic of all were the young people. Fanny Cavender who had been living at Roadside since her mother's death was engaged to Tom Parrish. During the first lonely winter evenings, they kept Lucretia company. While she sat by the library fire, Fanny would play the piano and Tom the flute. Sometimes Willie Davis brought out his violin and accompanied them. Then "You ought to hear their pretty music," Lucretia wrote.

Fanny and Tom had planned to be married on the Motts' wedding anniversary. After James's death, her aunts begged her to postpone the wedding.

"Nonsense," her grandmother said when she overheard a discussion. "Thou will do no such thing. 'Twill give me joy to share my happy day with you."

When the young couple exchanged vows in the parlor at Roadside on the 10th day of Fourth month, Lucretia wept unashamedly. "They are not tears of bitterness but of tenderness," she explained. "I'm remembering my blessings and the blessing of James's long life with me."

It didn't take long for her stubborn little chin to lose its wobbliness. Although she still mourned "the happy days of Roadside before the glory departed," her natural optimism asserted itself. By June she was riding in to Philadelphia for meetings. After a trip to New York in the fall she wrote Martha, "When you are going to Nantucket, let a body know and I'm your man!"

James had left almost $100,000, a considerable sum in 1868. Although Edward Hopper was executor of the estate, Lucretia took an interest in her business affairs. Her first impulse was to sell Roadside and move to a smaller place. "I should have more entirely a loose foot," she thought.

After more careful consideration, she decided to dispose of some of the fields that would no longer be used for farming. Offering lots at low prices to black war veterans who had trained at Camp William Penn, she was pleased when a black community grew up west of Old York Road. The community which is now just outside the Philadelphia city line is still called La Mott.

Swarthmore College was another piece of unfinished business that James had bequeathed to her. When it opened the year after his death, Tom helped her bring two oak trees from Roadside, trees that James had started from acorns. She planted the trees on the college grounds as a memorial to his interest in education. She hadn't planned to speak at the inaugural ceremonies, but finding that no woman was listed on the program, "I had to thrust in an improviso."

With Anna Hopper on the Board of Managers and grandchildren and great-grands enrolled as students, there soon seemed to be as many members of the Mott family at Swarth-

more as there once had been at Nine Partners. Lucretia
rode out to the campus often. On her wedding anniversary
in 1871, she gave the school a painting of William Penn
with the Indians. After its presentation, she stayed overnight to talk with the students and attend a stereopticon
lecture.

Unable to spend more than a fraction of her income on
herself, she gave the rest away—to Swarthmore, to her family, to old friends and good causes. She sent $100 to Boston
to an aging abolitionist who was sick. She paid Susan Anthony's expenses when she lectured on woman's rights, and
then mailed Susan "another ten for thy own personal use."

Her favorite local charity was the Stephen Smith Home
for Aged and Infirm Colored Persons which she and James
had help to establish. Even when she was older than many
of its inmates, she never failed to drive there the day before Christmas, bringing gingham aprons for the women
and handkerchiefs for the men, along with a wagonload of
turkeys and mince pies.

Although she was beginning to complain that her hand
trembled when she wrote, her family letters were as sprightly
as ever. Starting with a weather report—"it blows, it snows"
or "Springlike at last!"—she alternated sharp comments on
politics with accounts of the children who had "such a fire-
cracker time" on the Fourth of July. "Edward got a box of
torpedoes and a few pinwheels. If they have their eyes tomorrow we shall be thankful."

Still the big sister, she scolded Martha for writing with
pink ink on "fancy" paper. "I can't conceive what one of thy
age wants such paper and ink for. It may please foolish
children to have their initials on embossed paper and pay
accordingly, but give me black and white."

When Martha retorted with a criticism of the cut-open

envelopes she sometimes wrote on, Lucretia chuckled. "Aunt Martha has given me an added lecture on the cheapness of note paper," she told Patty. "One would suppose you had all learned by this time that the old lady chooseth to do as best suits her."

29. I Mean to Live As Long As I Can

*The striking traits of Lucretia's character are re-
markable energy that defies even time, unswerving
conscientiousness, and all those characteristics that
are summed up in the few words, love to man and
love to God.*

MARTHA WRIGHT, 1868

The days passed quickly. In the summer, Lucretia rose early
and went outdoors, enjoying the smell of the moist earth
before the hot sun dried it out. With a floppy sunbonnet on
her head and a basket over her arm, she picked peas or
brought in a quart of raspberries for her family to enjoy at
breakfast. When the orchard fruit was ripe, she arranged
apples and pears on the stone wall in front of the house so
passing children could find them.

In winter she was up before the sun. Building her own
fire in the library, she answered letters before the rest of
the household came downstairs. Afternoons were usually
spent with visitors. Although her children tried to protect
her from people like "that good uninteresting Methodist mis-
sionary" who stayed and stayed, she welcomed calls from
Garrison or Burleigh or McKim. "How sot Miller is against
women reformers—and men too, I guess," she reported to
Martha. "A change indeed, but we haven't a better talker
yet."

Often it was the women reformers themselves who came
to Roadside to talk over affairs of state. When Elizabeth
Stanton and Susan Anthony formed a National Woman Suf-

frage Association, Lucretia declined to become an officer. "My strength now is not mighty," she said. "I never expect to join another organization."

This resolve lasted for a few weeks. Then she asked Martha to attend a convention in Saratoga because "E. C. Stanton will need thee." Soon afterward Elizabeth and Susan allied themselves with Victoria Woodhull. Mrs. Woodhull was a beautiful woman, and a forceful advocate of woman's rights. It was rumored, however, that she believed in free love. When she agreed to speak at the Woman Suffrage meeting in 1871, the newspapers promptly labeled the meeting "The Free Love Convention."

Elizabeth needed Lucretia—and she came. Serene in her white cap and full-skirted drab gown, she sat next to Mrs. Woodhull on the platform, her presence guaranteeing the respectability of the gathering. Alas, the following year it appeared that the rumors about Mrs. Woodhull were true. When she became involved in a sensational scandal she was clapped into jail.

Although Elizabeth and Susan hastily disavowed her, Lucretia maintained that her imprisonment was a "hateful wrong." Still serene, she pointed out that the Vice-President of the United States and leading Congressmen were involved in a far more serious scandal. They had accepted bribes from a company that was bilking the government, but none of them were going to be prosecuted. "If all those greedy monopolizers can come off scot free," Lucretia said, "we needn't be too much afraid to give the Devil his due in other cases."

Nevertheless, when Victoria Woodhull wrote to her, she felt uncomfortable about replying. What could one say to an advocate of free love? "Thou must answer it, Edward," she begged. "I just don't know how."

Never robust, Lucretia continued to lose weight in the years after James's death. By 1872 she weighed only seventy-six pounds. Although she looked as if a puff of wind would blow her away, her vitality amazed everybody. Mariana described her arrival at the Hoppers one afternoon: "I must tell you how dear Mother came in from Roadside. Under that deceiving cloak of hers, which is supposed to be merely a covering for her little wire threads of legs, she carried eggs by the dozen, chickens and 'a little sweet piece of pickled pork,' mince pies, the vegetables of the season. She concealed how much of the way she had walked from the station or how broad a trail of dropped eggs she left behind her. But as she at last reached the house and tugged at the stiff bell cord, a big bottle of cream slipped from her tired hands. It smashed upon the top step, a libation at the threshold, but so much better in coffee. Wasn't that hard?"

Edward Davis, trying to take James's place as her escort, sometimes found it difficult to keep up with her. When she insisted on going to a meeting one snowy night, she said afterward, "I couldn't have reached the hall if not for Edward's strong arm." His comment was "Mother trotted me along!"

She trotted him along again in 1873 when she heard that President Grant was in the neighborhood. She had something to say to the President. Out in California, the Modoc Indians had resisted the Army's attempt to move them to a reservation. After months of fighting, their leader, Captain Jack, was caught. With eleven of his braves, he was sentenced to be hanged.

Learning that Grant was visiting her financier-neighbor, Jay Cooke, Lucretia reached for her bonnet. "I'm going to call on the President to plead for the lives of the condemned Indians," she announced.

"Mother, thou has no invitation," Edward protested. "Thou has not announced thy desire. Etiquette demands that thou send first to see if it will be agreeable for the President."

Lucretia frowned. "My visit is too urgent to wait on etiquette. I feel constrained to go now. If thou art willing to accompany me, will thou harness the horse?"

Edward harnessed the horse and drove her to the Cookes' mansion. She had a nodding acquaintance with the financier whose son visited Roadside to play with her grandchildren. When she gave her name at the door, she was quickly ushered in to see the President.

With her luminous gray eyes turned full force on Grant's face, Lucretia appealed for mercy for Captain Jack and his men. "Thou alone has the power to pardon them," she pointed out. "It is up to thee."

Grant listened thoughtfully. After reminding her that the whole country, North and South, was united in a wish to see the Indians punished, he leaned toward her. Speaking in a low voice, as if only for her ear, "Madam," he promised "they shall not all be executed."

The President kept his word. Although Captain Jack was hanged the lives of six of his men were spared.

President Grant's reaction to Lucretia Mott was not out of the ordinary. At eighty, she had become a legend. After all her years as the champion of unpopular causes, she was now universally beloved. Even strangers stopped her on the street to take her hand or whispered "God bless you!" as she went by.

She first noticed the change when she spoke at a meeting in New York with Sojourner Truth. Remembering the last time she and Sojourner had shared a platform, she told

Martha with some surprise, "People were very attentive and many expressed satisfaction and thanked me. Sojourner did very well. The audience was interested in her. Now I must collect my duds and be off to Boston."

In Boston it was the same thing. Try as she would to take a back seat, she couldn't enter a hall without being led to the dais and begged to say "just five words." "So the old goose did," she laughed at herself, "and such a huge bouquet they brought me."

When the Pennsylvania Abolition Society—the society that old Dr. Parrish had headed—celebrated its 100th anniversary, its members gave Lucretia a standing ovation. As the cheers subsided she responded in a voice tremulous with emotion:

> "I've heard of hearts unkind, kind words
> With coldness still returning
> Alas! the *gratitude* of man,
> Hath oftener left *me* mourning."

Long ago, George Combe had said that Lucretia had a large bump of approbation. Although she found it pleasant to be appreciated where she had once been shunned, some of the flattery left her squirming. After one flowery bit of oratory she murmured, "I'm a very much overrated woman. It's humiliating."

On another occasion when Maria read an article that praised her extravagantly—in the past tense—her lips twitched. "It's better not to be in a hurry with obituaries" she retorted.

As the years passed, she found herself outliving her contemporaries. She went to Nantucket when Nathaniel Barney died. She spoke at Thomas Garrett's funeral in Wilmington. She mourned Sumner, Charles Burleigh, then Garrison. Far harder to bear were the losses within her own family—Sister Elizabeth, Mariana, Anna, and, in 1875, Sister Martha.

Tears spotted the paper as she wrote Martha's daughter, "Now we have no lovely and loving letters from Auburn any more."

And still she continued to be active. In 1876 the United States was one hundred years old. To celebrate the occasion the government held a gigantic Centennial Exposition in Philadelphia. Fairmount Park, where James used to take visitors for First day drives, was transformed into a fairyland of glass and steel. The exhibition halls housed every new invention known to man from a gaudy marble soda fountain to Alexander Graham Bell's first crude telephone. Lucretia looked at a model of an oil well, thinking perhaps of Nantucket's whaling fleet which had finally been driven from the sea by the discovery of petroleum. She fingered a typewriter and marveled at a Pullman car that offered luxurious beds and hot dinners to travelers to the West.

The Centennial gave a breath-taking glimpse into the future, but nowhere in the 180 pavilions was there a record of woman's accomplishments. Even the Fourth of July ceremonies in the State House were to be an all-male affair. Disappointed by their exclusion, the National Woman Suffrage Association rented parlors on Chestnut Street. Susan Anthony manned the headquarters and Lucretia Mott acted as hostess to the thousands of women who came to Philadelphia.

On July 4, while the emperor of Brazil spoke in the State House, the women held their own meeting in a downtown church. In the crowded room, it was hard to see Lucretia when she rose to speak. Several people called, "Go up into the pulpit!"

As she climbed the winding staircase that led to the pulpit, the Hutchinsons, her Singing Yankee friends, started to sing "Nearer, My God, to Thee." Watching the slow as-cent of the frail, childlike figure, the women tearfully joined in the hymn.

Once again, it was a case of hurrying the obituaries. Lucretia spoke forcefully that day and continued to come in to Chestnut Street almost every morning, during a season so warm that Philadelphians for a generation afterward spoke of "as hot as the Centennial summer."

When a young woman offered her arm as they crossed the street together, Lucretia refused her help. "I'm not old enough for that," she grinned. "Don't thee be uneasy. I learned a long time ago to lean upon myself."

In August when the women's headquarters closed, she went to Nantucket. After the razzle-dazzle of the Centennial, it was a relief to return to the quiet little island. With a party of grandchildren and great-grands in tow, she visited her old home on Fair Street, and walked up Mill Hill to show them the windmill where she had once carried corn to be ground.

That summer was her farewell to Nantucket, but two years later she traveled to Rochester for the thirtieth anniversary of the woman's rights movement. As she finished speaking, she left the platform and walked slowly down the aisle shaking hands. Sensing that this was the last time they would see her, the audience rose in tribute. Frederick Douglass took her arm to say for everyone, "Goodbye, dear Lucretia, goodbye."

And still she continued. Birthdays brought letters from all sorts of people—a congratulatory message from Queen Victoria, a penciled note from a black scrubwoman, a thank-you from the North Pennsylvania Railroad conductors who had been helping her off the cars for so many years. Some letters asked for autographs and mottoes. Lucretia kept little slips of paper on which she patiently copied, "*Truth for au-*

thority, not authority for truth," the motto she had long ago
adopted as her own.

Friends found her in the library at Roadside, finishing
John Stuart Mill's autobiography, or resting her eyes by
cutting and sewing carpet rags. When she announced her
intention of making new carpets for each of her children,
Elizabeth Stanton scoured cellars and attics to collect an
enormous bundle of brightly colored rags. She sent them to
Lucretia with a rhyme:

> "Lucretia Mott, my dearest friend
> This day to you a box I send
> Containing gifts so bright and rare
> I warn you to unpack with care.
>
> Alas! my daughters and my nieces
> Who saved all these little pieces
> Would that they could see, I know,
> You, to whom these offerings go.
>
> I fancy in that Roadside home
> Your sitting with them all alone
> With artistic touch, in leisure hours
> Weaving anew their lives in flowers.
>
> Oftimes I have wished myself
> Some horrid man, a bird or elf,
> But now I'd gladly be a scarlet rag
> To live forever in thy carpet bag."

And still she continued. She went to Philadelphia for the
monthly meetings of the Peace Society and, in May 1880,
attended the yearly meeting of the Society of Friends.
"Yearly Meeting is over," Maria wrote Patty, "and our
bright young mother of eighty-seven none the worse for it.
She always did thrive on excitement. She spoke only a
short time but with unusual earnestness and feeling. I was
often entertained by the side remarks of those around. Once

someone directly behind me said to her companion, 'Well, Lucretia has outlived her persecutors.' There is no question but that our mother is better than she was a week ago. Now she wants to carry out her intention of going to Medford and Cambridge."

She never made the journey. Growing weaker during the summer, she spent more and more time in her room. She was dying, but she still greeted visitors eagerly, begging for news of the reform movements and of the exciting election campaign. On the day that James Garfield was elected the twentieth President of the United States, she struggled to sit up.

"I don't dread death," she told her family. "But remember that my life has been a simple one. Let simplicity mark the last done for me. I charge thee, do not forget."

On the 11th day of Eleventh month, 1880, Lucretia Mott died. More than a thousand people followed her plain walnut coffin from Roadside to the burying ground. A chill November wind blew, scattering dry leaves into the open grave.

"Will no one say anything?" a low voice asked.

"Who can speak?" another replied. "The preacher is dead!"

Lucretia Mott's Contemporaries

JOHN QUINCY ADAMS (1767–1848) Sixth President of the
United States, Adams served as Congressman from 1831
—48. In those years, he was the leader of the small anti-
slavery group in Congress and an eloquent defender of
the right of abolitionists to be heard.

SUSAN B. ANTHONY (1820–1906) A Quaker abolitionist and
schoolteacher, Susan Anthony joined Elizabeth Cady
Stanton in organizing the Women's Loyal League and
the National Woman Suffrage Association. Miss Anthony
was president of the National American Woman Suffrage
Association from 1892–1900.

CHARLES BURLEIGH (1810–78) A graduate of Yale, Burleigh
gave up a promising law career for the anti-slavery movement. A brilliant lecturer and writer, he was for many
years the editor of the *Pennsylvania Freeman.*

MARIA CHAPMAN (1806–85) Organizer of the Boston Female Anti-Slavery Society and of the Anti-Slavery Ba-
zaars held annually in Boston for more than twenty
years, Maria Chapman also edited *The Liberator* when
Garrison was ill or abroad. Blonde, blue-eyed Mrs. Chapman, as beautiful as she was clever, was called "the
coiled-up mainspring" of the anti-slavery movement.

LYDIA MARIA CHILD (1802–80) Until she wrote *An Appeal
in Behalf of That Class of Americans Called Africans*,
Lydia Maria Child was the most popular woman writer
in the United States. After that, bookstores refused to
carry her books, Southerners burned them, and the of-

ficers of the Boston Anthenaeum withdrew her card to
their library. Continuing to work for the anti-slavery
cause, Mrs. Child wrote more than thirty books and
pamphlets, in addition to editing the *National Anti-
Slavery Standard.*

THOMAS CLARKSON (1760–1846) An English abolitionist,
Clarkson was the first to call the attention of the world
to the horrors of the slave trade. His tireless agitation
led to the abolition of slavery in the British West Indies
in 1832.

ROBERT COLLYER (1823–1912) Starting life as a blacksmith, Robert Collyer became a Unitarian clergyman
and well-known lecturer and writer. Active in the reform
movements of his day, he was minister of the Church of
the Messiah in New York for nearly thirty years.

GEORGE COMBE (1788–1858) A Scottish phrenologist who
lectured in America, Combe was sympathetic to abolitionism and other reforms.

FREDERICK DOUGLASS (1817–95) The outstanding Negro
leader of the nineteenth century and one of the great
minds of his time, Douglass escaped from slavery in
1838. Joining the abolitionists as orator and editor of
North Star, he was also active in the woman's rights
movement. During the Civil War, he helped recruit regiments of Negro soldiers. After the war, while continuing
to lead the fight for civil rights, he became Recorder of
Deeds for the District of Columbia (1877–81) and Minister to Haiti (1889–91).

ROBERT AND SARAH DOUGLASS were the son and daughter
of a pioneer Negro educator who was one of the first
members of her race to join the Society of Friends. After
studying under Thomas Sully in Philadelphia and Lon-

don, Robert became a portrait painter of some renown. His sister, Sarah, was a schoolteacher and a member of the Philadelphia Female Anti-Slavery Society.

RALPH WALDO EMERSON (1803–82) Ralph Waldo Emerson was a poet, essayist, lecturer, and philosopher. His belief in the "infinite worthiness" of man and the responsibility of the individual toward society, helped shape the reform movements of the mid-nineteenth century.

JAMES FORTEN (1766–1842) A Negro spokesman, Forten fought in the American Revolution and afterward invented a device for handling sails that earned him more than $100,000. Author of an anti-slavery pamphlet, "Letters from a Man of Colour" (1813), he was one of the first supporters of Garrison's *Liberator*. His children and grandchildren were also active abolitionists.

WILLIAM H. FURNESS (1802–96) A graduate of Harvard, Furness became a Unitarian clergyman, author, and abolitionist. For fifty years he was minister of the First Unitarian Church in Philadelphia.

THOMAS GARRETT (1789–1871) A Quaker abolitionist living in the slave state of Delaware, Garrett helped 2700 slaves escape to freedom on the Underground Railroad.

WILLIAM LLOYD GARRISON (1805–79) An abolitionist editor, Garrison was a leader in reform movements throughout his life. His *Liberator*, founded in 1831, was the first U.S. newspaper to call for the immediate and unconditional abolition of slavery.

ELIAS HICKS (1748–1830) An eloquent Quaker preacher, Hicks was one of the first Americans to refuse to use cotton and sugar that had been grown by slaves. His criticism of Quakers who had forsaken the simple faith of an earlier day led the Society of Friends to divide into two groups, the Hicksites and the Orthodox.

THE HUTCHINSONS Calling themselves the "Singin' Yan-kees," the Hutchinson family—four brothers and a sister—gave concerts in the major cities of the U.S. and Europe in the middle of the nineteenth century. Allying them-selves with the anti-slavery movement and other reforms, they never failed to include abolitionist songs in their programs.

FANNY KEMBLE (1809–93) Actress Fanny Kemble was the darling of British and American theatergoers until her marriage in 1834 to Pierce Butler, a slaveowner. After a year on his plantation in Georgia, she joined the anti-slavery ranks. Her *Journal of a Residence on a Georgia Plantation in 1838–9* is still an important source of in-formation about slave life.

BENJAMIN LUNDY (1789–1839) A Quaker saddler, Lundy carried on a one-man crusade against slavery. Editor of *The Genius of Universal Emancipation,* and a founder of the free-produce movement, he also traveled to Haiti and Canada searching for places where freed slaves might live.

JAMES MILLER McKIM (1810–74) A leader of the abolition-ists in Pennsylvania, active in Freedmen's Relief Associ-ations during the Civil War, McKim was also a founder of the liberal weekly, *The Nation.* His daughter, Lucy, (1842–77) was an editor of the first collection of Negro spirituals.

THEODORE PARKER (1810–60) A Unitarian clergyman, Par-ker was an active abolitionist and reformer. In the 1850s when he was resisting the Fugitive Slave Law which threatened the freedom of every Negro in the North, he wrote his sermons with a sword and loaded pistol in his desk.

WENDELL PHILLIPS (1811–84) Handsome, well-born Wendell Phillips became the orator of the anti-slavery crusade. Known as "Abolition's golden trumpet," he also fought for woman's rights and for the rising trade union movement.

ROBERT PURVIS (1810–98) A Negro leader although he was so light in color that he might have passed for white, Purvis was a founder of the American Anti-Slavery Society and an organizer of the Underground Railroad in Pennsylvania. In the years before the Civil War, he helped more than 9000 slaves to escape.

ELIZABETH CADY STANTON (1815–1902) Leader in the woman's suffrage movement, Elizabeth Cady Stanton joined Lucretia Mott in calling the first woman's rights convention (1848). As journalist, lecturer, and organizer, Mrs. Stanton was in the forefront of the struggle for equal rights for women.

LUCY STONE (1818–93) One of the first woman college graduates, Lucy Stone became an abolitionist and woman's rights spokesman. When she married she continued to use her own name as a protest against the marriage laws which deprived women of their rights.

CHARLES SUMNER (1811–74) As U. S. Senator from Massachusetts from 1851–74, Charles Sumner was spokesman for the abolitionists and a leader in the struggle for Negro suffrage after the Civil War. His Civil Rights Bill was passed in 1875, shortly after his death.

SOJOURNER TRUTH (1797–1883) Born a slave in New York, Sojourner Truth traveled throughout the North and West preaching abolitionism and woman's rights. She was a powerful speaker, with a special facility for silencing hecklers. When one member of her audience said, "I don't care any more for your talk than I do for the bite of a flea," her answer was, "Perhaps not, but the Lord willing, I'll keep you scratching."

JOHN GREENLEAF WHITTIER (1807–92) A New England Quaker, John Greenleaf Whittier was the poet laureate of the abolitionist movement. A delegate to the first Anti-Slavery Convention, he edited the *Pennsylvania Freeman* and the *National Era,* anti-slavery weeklies. In addition to his anti-slavery poems, he wrote such popular favorites as "Barbara Frietchie," "The Barefoot Boy," and "Snow-Bound."

Acknowledgments

My deepest thanks go to Dr. Frederick B. Tolles of the Friends Historical Library of Swarthmore College, and to Mrs. Margaret S. Grierson and Miss Elizabeth S. Duvall of the Sophia Smith Collection in the Smith College Library for their friendly assistance while I was reading the Mott family letters in the Swarthmore and Smith libraries. I should also like to thank Dr. Tolles for his critical reading of my manuscript.

Others who helped me to locate unpublished material about Lucretia Mott include Mr. R. N. Williams of the Historical Society of Pennsylvania, Miss Agnes Campbell of the New York Yearly Meeting of the Society of Friends, Miss Mary Ogilvie of the Philadelphia Yearly Meeting, and Miss Ethel Anderson of the Nantucket Historical Association. In Poughkeepsie, Mr. and Mrs. Charles Hutton welcomed me to Oakwood School, the successor to Nine Partners, and loaned me books and sketches of the original building. On Nantucket, Will Gardner, the island's historian, told me stories of the Coffin family and Harold Lindley, proprietor of Ships Inn, showed me through Lucretia Mott's home on Fair Street which he and his family now occupy. For all of these courtesies, many thanks.

I am also indebted to Gilbert A. Cam for the use of the New York Public Library's Frederick Lewis Allen Room, and particularly to Miss Mary Lyon of the Rye Free Reading Room for the cheerfulness and dispatch with which she obtained books for me through the library's inter-branch loan facilities. Special thanks should also go to Mrs. Rhoda Jenkins, great-granddaughter of Elizabeth Cady Stanton, her mother, Mrs. Nora Barney, and the Rye Friends Meeting, for lending me books which I kept far too long.

I should like to add a note of gratitude to Barnard College which is celebrating its 75th Anniversary in 1964. As I complete this biography of a pioneer American woman it seems particularly appropriate to pay tribute to Barnard, a pioneer in the field of higher education for women.

Bibliography

The most important source of information for this biography of Lucretia Mott are her family letters which are on file at the Friends Historical Library of Swarthmore College, Swarthmore, Pa.; the Sophia Smith Collection, Smith College Library, Northampton, Mass.; the Nantucket Historical Association, Nantucket, Mass.; and the New York Public Library.

Of almost equal value are *James and Lucretia Mott*, a biography written by their granddaughter, Anna Davis Hallowell, published by Houghton Mifflin in 1884, and *Lucretia Mott* by Otelia Cromwell, published by Harvard University Press, 1958. I have also consulted the following books and manuscripts:

LUCRETIA MOTT AND HER FAMILY

Bolton, Sarah K. *Lives of Girls Who Became Famous,* New York, 1886.

Burnett, Constance B. *Five For Freedom,* New York, 1953.

────*Lucretia Mott,* Indianapolis, 1951.

Coffin, Robert P. Tristram. *Ballads of Square-Toed Americans,* New York, 1933.

Cornell, Thomas C. *Adam and Anne Mott. Their Ancestors and Descendants,* Poughkeepsie, 1890.

Furness, W. H. *God and Immortality. A Discourse In Memory of Lucretia Mott,* Philadelphia, 1881.

Grew, Mary. *James Mott,* Philadelphia, 1868.

Hale, Sara Josepha. *Woman's Record,* New York, 1855.

Hallowell, William Penrose. *Record of a Branch of the Hallowell Family,* Philadelphia, 1893.

Hare, Lloyd C. M. *The Greatest American Woman: Lucretia Mott,* New York, 1937.

Mott, James. *Observations on the Education of Children,* New York, 1816.

Mott, James. *Three Months in Great Britain,* Philadelphia, 1841.

Rosenberger, Homer T. "Montgomery County's Greatest Lady: Lucretia Mott" in *Bulletin of the Historical Society of Montgomery County,* VI, 1948.

Smith, Elizabeth Oakes. "Lucretia Mott" in *Potter's American Monthly*, March 1881.

Tolles, Frederick B., ed. *Slavery and "The Woman Question". Lucretia Mott's Diary of Her Visit to Great Britain to Attend the World's Anti-Slavery Convention of 1840*. Haverford, Pa. and London, 1952.

Lucretia Mott, Philadelphia, 1880.

——"Personal Reminiscences of Lucretia Mott" in *Harper's Weekly*, December 4, 1880.

SOCIETY OF FRIENDS

Brinton, Howard. *Friends for 300 Years*, New York, 1952.

Drake, Thomas. *Quakers and Slavery in America*, New Haven, 1950.

Forbush, Bliss. *Elias Hicks, Quaker Liberal*, New York, 1956.

Jones, Rufus. *Later Periods of Quakerism*, London, 1921, 2 vol.

Parrish, Edward. *An Essay on Education in the Society of Friends*, New York, 1866.

Sellers, Sarah Pennock. *David Sellers*, Philadelphia, 1927.

Sykes, John. *The Quakers*, London, 1858.

Tolles, Frederick B. *Meeting House and Counting House. The Quaker Merchants of Colonial Philadelphia*, Chapel Hill, 1948.

Woolman, John. *Journal of John Woolman*, Philadelphia, 1898.

Wright, Edward Needles. *Conscientious Objectors in the Civil War*, New York, 1961.

NANTUCKET AND BOSTON

Baker, Louise S. *Eunice Hussey*, Nantucket, 1938.

Chamberlain, Samuel. *Nantucket*, New York, 1955.

Early, Eleanor. *An Island Patchwork*, Cambridge, 1941.

Gardner, Helen. "Cent Schools" in *Proceedings of the Nantucket Historical Association*, July 21, 1908.

Gardner, Will. *The Coffin Saga*, Cambridge, 1949.

Larcom, Lucy. *A New England Girlhood*, New York, 1961.

Morrison, Samuel E. *Maritime History of Massachusetts*, Cambridge, 1921.

Stackpole, Edouard A. *The Sea-Hunters*, New York, 1953

Starbuck, Alexander. *History of Nantucket*, Boston, 1924.

Stevens, William O. *Nantucket, The Far Away Island*, New York, 1936.

Wolfe, Reese. *Yankee Ships*, Indianapolis, 1953.

Writers Program of the WPA. *Boston Looks Seaward*, Boston, 1941.

NINE PARTERS

Carmer, Carl. *The Hudson,* New York, 1939.

Cowper, William. *Poetical Works,* New York, n.d.

Dillwyn, George. *Occasional Reflections Offered Principally for the Use of Schools,* 1815.

Holbrook, Stewart. *The Old Post Road,* New York, 1962.

King, Charles D., Jr. *History of Education in Dutchess County 1716–1959,* Cape May, N.J., 1959.

McCracken, Henry Noble. *Blithe Dutchess,* New York, 1958.

McGonegal, Esther. "Nine Partners Boarding School" in *Bulletin of Friends Historical Society,* November, 1920.

Reynolds, Helen. "Nine Partners Patent, Nine Partners Meeting and Nine Partners School" in *Year Book Dutchess County Historical Society,* Vol. 20, 1935.

Talcott, Joseph. *Memoirs and Letters of Joseph Talcott,* Auburn, 1855.

Wakefield, Priscilla. *Domestic Recreation: Or Dialogues Illustrative of Natural and Scientific Subjects,* Philadelphia, 1805.

Wilstach, Paul. *Hudson River Landings,* Indianapolis, 1933.

Manuscripts: Minutes of New York Yearly Meeting and Nine Partners School Committee, Society of Friends, 1795–1810.

PHILADELPHIA

Oberholtzer, Ellis Paxson. *Philadelphia, A History of the City and Its People,* Philadelphia, 1912. 4 vol.

Trollope, Frances. *Domestic Manners of the Americans,* New York, 1949.

Writers Program of the WPA. *Pennsylvania, A Guide to the Keystone State,* Philadelphia, 1940.

THE ANTI-SLAVERY MOVEMENT

Adams, Alice Dana. *The Neglected Period of Anti-Slavery in America 1808–1831,* Boston, 1908.

Allen, William F., Charles P. Ware, Lucy McKim Garrison. *Slave Songs of the United States,* New York, 1867.

Aptheker, Herbert. *A Documentary History of the Negro People of the United States,* New York, 1951.

Armstrong, Margaret. *Fanny Kemble,* New York, 1938.

A Southerner. *Sketches of the Higher Classes of Colored Society in Philadelphia,* 1841.

Barnes, Gilbert H. and Dwight L. Dumond. *Letters of Theodore*

D. Weld, Angelina Grimke Weld and Sarah Grimke 1822–44, New York, 1934.

Billington, Ray Allen, ed. The Journal of Charlotte Forten, New York, 1953.

Birney, Catherine H. Sarah and Angelina Grimke, Boston, 1885.

Brink, Carol. Harps in the Wind, New York, 1947.

Chace, Elizabeth B. and Lucy B. Lovell. Two Quaker Sisters, New York, 1937.

Chadwick, John White, ed. A Life for Liberty, New York, 1899.

Child, Lydia M. Isaac T. Hopper, Boston, 1853.

——Letters, Cambridge, 1883.

Coffin, Levi. Reminiscences of Levi Coffin, Cincinnati, 1876.

Douglass, Frederick. Life and Times of Frederick Douglass, Hartford, Conn., 1881.

DuBois, W. E. B. The Philadelphia Negro, Philadelphia, 1899.

——The Suppression of the African Slave Trade to the United States, New York, 1954.

Dumond, Dwight Lowell. Antislavery, Ann Arbor, 1961.

——Antislavery Origins of the Civil War in the United States, Ann Arbor, 1959.

Fauset, Arthur Huff. Sojourner Truth, Chapel Hill, 1938.

Filler, Louis. The Crusade Against Slavery, 1830–60, New York, 1960.

Foner, Philip. Life and Writings of Frederick Douglass, New York, 1950–55, 4 vol.

Furness, William H. Recollections of Seventy Years, Philadelphia, 1895.

Garrison, W. P. and F. J. William Lloyd Garrison, Cambridge, 1894, 4 vol.

Grimke, Archibald. William Lloyd Garrison, New York, 1891.

Higginson, Thomas Wentworth. Letters and Journals, Cambridge, 1921.

Holmes, John Haynes. The Life and Letters of Robert Collyer, New York, 1917, 2 vol.

Johnson, Oliver. William Lloyd Garrison and His Times, Boston, 1879.

Jordan, Philip. Singin' Yankees, Minneapolis, 1946.

Korngold, Ralph. Two Friends of Man, Boston, 1950.

Lowell, James Russell. The Poetical Works of James Russell Lowell, Cambridge, 1890.

Lundy, Benjamin. The Life, Travels and Opinions of Benjamin Lundy, Philadelphia, 1847.

May, Samuel. *Some Recollections of our Antislavery Conflict*, Boston, 1869.

Mott, Lucretia. *A Sermon to the Medical Students*, Philadelphia, 1849.

——"Diversities" in *The Liberty Bell*, Boston, 1844.

National Anti-Slavery Standard, October 1859–February 1860.

Needles, Edward. *An Historical Memoir of the Pennsylvania Society for Promoting the Abolition of Slavery*, Philadelphia, 1848.

Nuermberger, Ruth. *The Free Produce Movement*, Durham, N.C., 1942.

Nye, Russell B. *Fettered Freedom*, East Lansing, Mich., 1949.

Pickard, Samuel. *Life and Letters of John Greenleaf Whittier*, Cambridge, 1894.

Pillsbury, Parker. *Acts of Anti-Slavery Apostles*, Concord, N.H., 1883.

Powell, Aaron. *Personal Reminiscences of the Anti-Slavery Movement and Other Reforms and Reformers*, New York, 1899.

Purvis, Robert. *Speeches and Correspondence of Robert Purvis*. Published by the request of the Afro-American League, n.d.

Quarles, Benjamin. *Frederick Douglass*, Washington, 1948.

Redpath, James. *The Public Life of Capt. John Brown*, Boston, 1860.

Rush, N. Orwin. "Lucretia Mott and the Philadelphia Antislavery Fairs" in *Bulletin of Friends Historical Association*, Autumn, 1946.

Sherwin, Oscar. *Prophet of Liberty. The Life and Times of Wendell Phillips*, New York, 1958.

Siebert, Wilbur H. *The Underground Railroad from Slavery to Freedom*, New York, 1899.

Smedley, R. C. *History of the Underground Railroad*, Lancaster, Pa., 1883.

Still, William. *The Underground Railroad*, Philadelphia, 1872.

Turner, Edward R. *The Negro in Pennsylvania, 1639–1861*, Washington, 1911.

Wheatley, Vera. *The Life and Work of Harriet Martineau*, Fair Lawn, N.J., 1957.

Whittier, John Greenleaf. *Complete Poems*, Vol III, Cambridge, 1895.

Yates, Elizabeth. *Prudence Crandall*, New York, 1955.

——*Appeal of Forty Thousand Citizens Threatened with Disfranchisement to the People of Pennsylvania*, Philadelphia, 1838.

——*History of Pennsylvania Hall which was Destroyed by a Mob on the 17th of May, 1838*, Philadelphia, 1838.

——*Proceedings of the National Anti-Slavery Convention*, New York, 1833.

——*Appeal to the Women of the Nominally Free States Issued by an Anti-Slavery Convention of American Women*, New York, 1837.

——*Proceedings of the Anti-Slavery Convention of American Women*, Philadelphia, 1838.

Manuscripts: Records of the Philadelphia Female Anti-Slavery Society, 1833–1870; Minute Book of Vigilant Committee of Philadelphia.

WOMAN'S RIGHTS

Anthony, Katharine. *Susan B. Anthony*, New York, 1954.

Anthony, Susan B. and Ida Husted Harper. *History of Woman Suffrage*, Vol IV, Rochester, 1902.

Finley, Ruth. *Lady of Godey's*, New York, 1931.

Flexner, Eleanor. *Century of Struggle*, Cambridge, 1959.

Irwin, Inez Haynes. *Angels and Amazons*, New York, 1940.

Lutz, Alma. *Susan B. Anthony: Rebel, Crusader, Humanitarian*, Boston, 1959.

——*Created Equal: A Biography of Elizabeth Cady Stanton*, New York, 1940.

Stanton, Elizabeth Cady. *Eighty Years and More*, New York, 1898.

——Susan Anthony and Mathilda Gage, eds. *History of Woman Suffrage*, Vol I & II, Rochester, 1881.

Stanton, Theodore and Harriot Stanton Blatch, eds. *Elizabeth Cady Stanton as Revealed in Her Letters, Diary and Reminiscences*, New York, 1922, 2 vols.

Suhl, Yuri. *Ernestine L. Rose and the Battle for Human Rights*, New York, 1959.

Whitton, Mary O. *These Were the Women*, New York, 1954.

OTHER REFORMS AND REFORMERS

Commager, Henry. *The Era of Reform 1830–60.*, New York, 1960.

Curti, Merle. *The Growth of American Thought*, New York, 1951.

——*Peace or War*, New York, 1936.

Rusk, Ralph L., ed. *The Letters of Ralph Waldo Emerson*, Vol III, New York, 1939.

Sargent, Mrs. John T. *Sketches and Reminiscences of the Radical Club*, Boston, 1880.

Tharp, Louise. *The Peabody Sisters of Salem*, Boston, 1950.

——*Until Victory*, Boston, 1953.

GENERAL HISTORIES

Crow, Carl. *The Great American Customer*, New York, 1943.

Franklin, John Hope. *From Slavery to Freedom*, New York, 1956.
Higginson, Thomas Wentworth. *History of the United States*, New
    York, 1905.
Hughes, Langston and Milton Meltzer. *A Pictorial History of the
    Negro in America*, New York, 1956.
Parrington, Vernon L. *Main Currents in American Thought*, New
    York, 1927.
Schlesinger, Arthur. *A Political and Social History of the United
    States, 1829–1925*, New York, 1925.
Seldes, Gilbert. *The Stammering Century*, New York, 1928.

About the Author

DORTHY STERLING is a native New Yorker who lives now in Rye, New York, with her husband and children. She was educated at Wellesley and Barnard Colleges and worked at Time, Inc., before leaving to devote herself to her family and her writing.

Not only is Mrs. Sterling a good writer, but she is also a painstaking and thorough researcher (the work on *Lucretia Mott* took two years). Mrs. Sterling has written books for all ages, and in addition to her highly praised non-fiction books for young people, she has proved her storytelling ability many times, with a long list of fiction, mysteries, and scientific books to her credit.

Fortunately for us, before the latest Sterling book is off the press, there is usually a new one in the planning stage.